Rarely Well-Behaved

◆

Rarely Well-Behaved

◆

A Short Story Collection

Phyllis Anne Duncan

Writers Club Press
San Jose New York Lincoln Shanghai

Rarely Well-Behaved
A Short Story Collection

Writers Club Press
an imprint of iUniverse.com, Inc.

For information address:
iUniverse.com, Inc.
5220 S 16th, Ste. 200
Lincoln, NE 68512
www.iuniverse.com

ISBN: 0-595-15164-7

Printed in the United States of America

Dedication

◆

To my maternal grandmother. Only in death could she find the happiness that eluded her in life.

To Vera McInnes, a teacher who first told me it was all right to imagine other worlds and places and to write what was in my heart. I wish she could have been here to see what that encouragement wrought.

For Beth, Megan, Andrea, Jared, Sarah, and David—the next generation.

"Well-behaved women rarely make history."

Laurel Thatcher Ulrich

Contents

◆

Foreword

◆

Brace yourself.

The stories you are about to read are **not** politically correct. They are not debates. They are not trials, and, as you read them, you will not be permitted to confront the witnesses who testify against your personal point of view. Both sides have **already** been heard, the verdicts are in, and the jurors are sleeping soundly.

You have arrived at the sentencing phase.

Mind you, none of this means that justice is avoided in Phyllis Duncan's *oeuvre*. Quite the contrary. All due process has been accorded to the parties in her fiction. No one herein is going to get something they don't deserve, and no cheap literary tricks are used to make the inequitable seem fair. Everyone she presents has *earned* what they get.

You may not agree. You have that right, but you didn't write this book. These are stories like you haven't seen in a while. These are not the cozy tales of people learning from their mistakes. Instead, you are going to see what might happen to characters who have **failed** to learn. And, in some cases, you won't like it.

But, looked at as it should be, that's a treat. The world is full of fine books and stories that reinforce the sweet notion that there is always a soft pillow to land on. It's rare, nowadays, to be reminded that, when we fall, it might be onto something **hard**. Ms. Duncan isn't ready to let us forget that. Yet, that's not to say she's about to bludgeon you with nothing but morbid lessons from the hard-knock school. Some folks can bounce off granite, if they have to, as you're about to see.

So, you don't have to like, or even agree with, the form her justice takes to learn a lesson or two from these pages. And, you should know, you're reading the works of a teacher. Some demand that their lessons be learned. Others, perhaps a little more secure about their own beliefs, merely offer to help you understand how one set of conclusions can be drawn, letting you pursue others once you've learned how to do it.

More than a quarter-century has passed since Ms. Duncan was my teacher. Then, as now, she was visible to us all mostly by contrast. Most of our teachers tried to tell us what to think. Some of the rest professed to teach us how but hid their own thoughts, which is a maddeningly impotent pedagogy. But, different from the others, Phyllis Duncan had a few thoughts of her own, and, by gum, we were going to know what they were and how she came to possess them. You could share them if you wanted to, or you could believe something else. Regardless, you were at least going to be exposed to the **whole** of an intellectual inquiry, including its outcome. For a young man about to drive, vote, and drink too much beer, some contact with someone who both believed the impossible and who **had reasons to do so** was a sobering experience. That experience taught me something, and—she's waited a long time to read this—it made me think.

Now, it's your turn. Remember, these are the words of someone **with a point of view**. Your approval thereof is not required. But, you are not merely going to be asked a series of Socratic questions. She's not that kind of teacher. You are about to be given some answers.

Brace yourself.

Stevens R. Miller
Ashburn, Virginia
September 2000

Preface

◆

These stories reflect my turn to fiction after many years of writing technical documents and other, aviation-related non-fiction. They coincide as well with a growth and discovery period in my own life and deal with themes important to me—choice, barriers, feminism. They also show the result of the evolution of two characters who are my foils. In between writing these stories, I wrote a novel, which is yet to be published, about the 1995 bombing of the Alfred P. Murrah Federal Building in Oklahoma City, Oklahoma. In Part 3 of this book, the characters will make occasional references to events in this work. Names have been changed to protect the innocent—and the guilty.

Phyllis Anne Duncan
Alexandria, Virginia
September 11, 2000

Acknowledgements

◆

I would like to acknowledge my family for providing the stuff of which stories are told and the family legends passed along, which I have embellished. My thanks to my friends, neighbors, teachers, professors, former students, and co-workers for their support and encouragement; as well to Marti Attoun and the Long Ridge Writers Group. My gratitude to the love of my life for his patience and belief in me.

Chronology

———————————◆———————————

The stories in Parts One and Two I wrote between 1994 and 1995. The stories in Part Three were written between 1998 and the present. The three-year gap represents the time spent researching and writing my first and as yet unpublished novel. The stories themselves take place anywhere between the 1930's and the present.

PART ONE

---◆---

*Family, or You Can't
Choose Your Relatives*

Introduction

———— ◆ ————

Every family has its stories, its trials and tribulations. Growing up, I thought that I must have the strangest family on the face of the earth. I was wrong. Dysfunction is the norm, and finally I can look back on the family history and accept it, occasionally even have a laugh.

"Choices" was written in 1993 in memory of the 20th anniversary of my grandmother's death. She was a remarkable woman who was born just after mankind first flew and died shortly after we walked on the moon. When I read Angela's Ashes *by Frank McCourt, I was, in a sense, relieved that my grandmother hadn't been the only one to live such a hard, painful life. Despite that, she never ran out of love and was a refuge at times for others' pain, including my own.*

"Going Home" is based on an actual event which took place in the early 1940's, a family legend I had heard many times. It became apocryphal, and its implications were not apparent for a long, long time. I owe my life to the young man's failure to kill: He was my father.

In "Fences" I tried to look at a much-disliked member of my family from her point of view. She left so much maladjustment in her wake that I realized there had to be another side to her. Though this portrayal is based in fact, it is a highly fictionalized portrait of an aunt who alienated everyone who should have loved and supported her.

My youth was spent in a world where your good name was everything and your accomplishments counted for little, particularly if you were female. I've single-handedly tried to reverse that in the way I live my life and by writing about things—as with "What's in a Name?"—that would scandalize my old-line Virginia family. Is that passive-aggressive? I hope so, because as the epigraph to this book intimates, I'm destined to make history.

I'm an unapologetic liberal, and the story, "Justice," came out of a debate over the death penalty. It is entirely fiction, and I've never been confronted with the loss of a loved one by murder. When I make my views on capital punishment known, the inevitable question posed to me is, "But what if someone you love is murdered?" I don't believe in state-sanctioned murder, but I do believe that what goes around comes around.

Choices

◆

I have no pictures of my grandmother as a child or a young woman, but a favorite is one taken in her early years as a matron—her late 30's, early 40's. It is a formal pose, hair in a chignon but wavy about her face; she is unsmiling. That is the only hint that she already had survived a brutal marriage and buried an infant son. In my memories, though, she is ever-smiling, talking about "my babies," the ones she birthed and the ones she midwifed.

That picture also doesn't hint of the choices my grandmother made, choices she began making early in her life. Some she made freely, some from necessity. (So, that begs the question, can a choice made from necessity really be a choice?) Her first husband was one made from necessity. Of my grandfather I know little. His name was a subject not to be brought up in front of her or my mother. Only an uncle, his namesake and physical double, provided a few details, though nothing more out of deference to his mother and sister. This near-stranger whose genes I carry is an unknown, except for the fact that his family and my grandmother's decided when he was 34 and she was 17 that she would be a settling influence on him. She married him because her father said she had to. It was 1920. Although she had completed a course in nursing, pursuing a career was not a choice she could freely make. Her "choice" was to go from her father's house to her husband's.

Because she had raised her motherless siblings and the half-siblings from her father's second marriage, she saw, oddly enough, her own marriage as an escape from drudgery. But that drudgery had taught her how to efficiently manage a household while doing her nursing on the side. However, her attempts at stabilizing my grandfather were met with his increased drinking and, ultimately, battering. When she caught a fever from a patient and began to lose her hearing, my grandfather refused to allow her to tell anyone. If people knew she was going deaf, they wouldn't hire her, and her nursing was now their only source of income—his profession being spending his time and her money at the local public house.

In time, they had a son, dutifully named after his father, and a daughter, named after the mother my grandmother had lost as a six-year old. A second son died of pneumonia after my grandfather drank up the money that was supposed to buy the winter's coal. To his credit (he is given so little), he was appropriately chagrined and offered to make a new start. Fortunately, my grandmother had a choice in the matter of how and where a new beginning could occur. A newly widowed friend of hers who had made a good marriage to a wealthy businessman in America offered to pay passage for my grandmother, grandfather, and the two children so the friend would have companionship in the new country. Eventually, this largess was extended to my great-grandfather, his second wife, and all my grandmother's siblings. They all "came over on the boat" in 1929 at the behest of this widow with nine children of her own. (This beneficent friend was to become my paternal grandmother, but that's another story.)

My grandfather's new start, unfortunately, was short-lived, but my grandmother, now almost entirely deaf, quickly learned to lip-read and established an association with one of the two local doctors. Through this doctor, she faced another choice. The doctor's women patients were often faced with pregnancies, which, for a variety of reasons, they wanted ended. In the 1930's a doctor caught performing abortions lost his license and suffered incarceration. (Now they face harassment and death at the hands of so-called pro-lifers.) At anywhere from $50 to $100 a procedure, the money appealed to my grandmother who had two young children to feed and clothe and an alcoholic husband to keep in drink. The doctor trained her, gave her the appropriate instruments and medications, and announced that if she were caught he would disavow any knowledge of her activities. The choice was easy; she needed the money. She freely chose to help rural women end unwanted or dangerous pregnancies. Because she had been a Protestant in Ireland, she had knowledge of birth control, and she gave instruction in that—also illegal then in Virginia.

In the 1970's when she finally confided this to me shortly after the Roe vs. Wade Supreme Court decision and only months before her death, she also confided one other choice she freely made, one that directly affected me.

The rich and poor women of Culpeper County, Virginia, she helped to abort because she felt they shouldn't have to give birth if they chose not to—and because they paid her well. But when her married daughter asked for an abortion because she didn't want to share her husband with her unborn child—me—my grandmother refused. My mother's subsequent attempts at Lysol douches and pitching herself down stairs failed (I'm still stubborn and pro-choice), and my grandmother kept up her distaff profession until only a few years before she died. She never lost a single mother; indeed, some of them later gave birth to babies which my grandmother delivered. Some call her, even now, a murderer; her patients called her a savior. She considered herself neither. She offered what she rarely could take advantage of—choice.

I believe her final choice came on the night she died. She was in robust health for 70—a touch of arthritis, occasional aches and pains, mild high blood pressure. After the death of her beloved second husband on

December 22, 1951, she often said, "I just want to go to sleep one night and not wake up."

On December 22, 1973, Maggie Marie Brown Pierce Smith chose to do just that.

Going Home

◆

The young man was determined. This was evident from the purposefulness of his stride, the set of his brow. He had walked nearly nine miles in the dark over cattle paths and fences. He had 10 more miles to go. Ten more miles and a man would die.

The young man—a boy of 15, really—had been walking for just over two hours. He figured that in two and a half or three more, he would be at his mother's house, his dead father's house, where his stepfather lived. By midnight, he should be there, and by midnight, his stepfather would be dead.

Long walks usually give one time to think, to reconsider. Hot heads have cooled considerably in the time it takes to reach the object of one's anger. Perhaps this boy's Scottish stubbornness was to blame, but his anger had abated none during his walk. It still flared as brightly as it had when he had overheard his oldest brother relating to a cousin how their drunken stepfather had beaten their mother for her failure to get dinner before him as quickly as he thought she should. No one had seen him listening; no one had seen him take the rifle from its rack and the ammunition from its shelf.

If I had been there, he thought, I could have stopped the bastard.

But he wasn't there. None of her first 10 children was there. The older ones were married and starting families of their own, but the younger ones had all been put out to relatives at the demand of their stepfather.

"By God, this is my house now," he had raged to his wife, "and only Smith children will live here. None of your brats with their high and mighty airs. You're just a farmer's wife now."

And so, at the age of 12, the young man had been forced out of the second home he had known.

He barely remembered the first, and some said he shouldn't be able to remember it at all. He was a few weeks older than two and still in baby dresses when his father died of a stroke. Yet, he could remember being held by the old man who had fathered him at the age of 70, he could remember the crying and wailing after the man's death, and he could remember being tied in his bed to keep him from following the cars for the funeral. He had been so young when his mother married his coarse stepfather that everyone assumed he would think of that man as his father. But he never had; he never would. He nurtured the scant memories of his own father, and they had comforted him during his stepfather's most egregious behavior.

I am not that man's son, he would think over and over and be relieved at the knowledge.

On the day that he and two brothers and a sister packed what clothes they were allowed to take, he looked at his mother, expecting her to say something, to tell them to go through the motions while her husband slept off his drunken pronouncement. But she had said nothing, her face unreadable. Others would say they saw relief there.

Every day for the past three years, the boy hoped to return to her, but none of them had been allowed even to enter the yard of their former home. Their mother visited them all periodically and queried about schoolwork but refused to answer the question whether it was spoken or not: When can I come home?

When the boy finally reached the crest of a hill overlooking his mother's house, he paused in his uncompromising trek to catch his breath. He needed to calm the frantic beating of his heart his exertion had caused; he didn't want his hands to shake and spoil his aim when he pulled the trigger.

In the white farmhouse, a light burned in one window, the parlor. His stepfather would be sitting there, drinking still. The boy's mother would be sitting with her husband, unable to retire to bed until he passed out and she carried him to bed.

A voice in the boy's head said, you're about to shoot a drunken man. Aloud, he whispered, "No, I'm about to shoot a drunken son of a bitch."

His breathing and heartbeat now normal, the boy inhaled deeply, with renewed purpose, and strode down the hill to the farmhouse's front door. He barely remembered entering the house and passing through the hallway to the parlor at the rear. He stepped inside and looked to the corner, knowing what he would find.

His stepfather sat in a battered armchair. A bottle of whiskey with only a dram left in it sat on a table beside him. He clutched a glassful in a beefy hand, and his round face was flushed, his gray eyes bloodshot and bleary. He had trouble focusing on the boy when he entered, but as the rifle came up to the boy's shoulder, its barrel aimed true at its target, he became half-sober and laughed.

"Well, boy, you gonna shoot me?" he drawled.

The boy did not respond but laid his cheek against the rifle's stock, aiming down the barrel as his oldest brother had taught him.

"You don't have the balls, boy. I'm not afraid of you."

Don't answer, don't talk, the voice inside the boy's head said. Get it done.

"Go ahead, boy. Shoot. Did you remember to load it?" The man laughed again, and the boy focused sharper at the bead at the end of the rifle's barrel, "setting" it in the notch of the sight. Blurred beyond the barrel's end was the fleshy bulk of his stepfather. The boy's finger moved to the trigger, which slipped easily behind the bend of the first joint of his index finger.

Take a deep breath and hold it, his brother's instructions echoed, then squeeze, don't pull, the trigger. His finger began to tighten.

The hazy image of his stepfather disappeared, replaced by the faded print of a woman's dress. The boy looked up. Between him and his target stood his mother. The right side of her face was miserably bruised, one lip swollen and cut. The boy's anger deepened.

"Move, Mother," he said.

"No, son," she said. "I can't let you do it."

"Then, leave the room."

"And get what? A dead husband and a son in the electric chair. Put the gun down, son."

The gun slid from his shoulder to hang uselessly in his hands. He stopped fighting his tears, held for three years, and let them fall. "Why, Mother, why?"

"I was a young woman married to an old man. Now, I'm married to a man my own age. You're too young to understand this now."

"Come away with me, please."

She tried to smile, but her split lip was too painful. "I'm this man's wife. My place is here, and you have your whole life ahead of you. You can't end it here."

"I'll only end his."

"The law won't see it that way. The state will wait until you're 18 and execute you for killing an unarmed drunk in his own house. I want to know your wife and hold your children."

Angrily, he said, "I won't make my children leave home."

The woman stared at him, not like a mother at all. "Understand this," she said. "I love him. You kill him, you kill me."

The tears flowed again as the boy shook his head, trying to deny her truth. The gun clattered to the floor as he blindly sought his way out of the house he no longer wanted to return to. The last thing he heard before he went out into the cool night was his stepfather's laughter.

And 40 years later when the life the boy took was his own, no one could answer why.

Fences

◆

The woman clutched the planking of a white picket fence, planted her feet firmly, and hauled backwards, applying the considerable strength of her 180 pounds. Wood splintered and shards flew; nails at first held, then released with a rusty screech. The plank came free. Through the sweat and the strands of hair hanging limply across her face, she grinned with pure pleasure. Without looking, she tossed the plank over her shoulder. It landed amid the embers of its companions and began to burn.

When the planking was all down, she worked away at the horizontal supports until they, too, were part of the fire, their protests sharp pops and cracks as paint bubbled and long buried pockets of resin exploded in the heat. Only the posts remained. The woman strode with intent toward the first in the line of sturdy posts. She embraced it like a lover and began to rock it back and forth. By the force of her will and the strength of her determination, she loosened the dirt that had held it in place for decades. She squatted, gripped tighter, and heaved upward, freeing the post from the ground. One by one, the posts mutely joined the fire, now a blaze whose smoke eddied skyward.

Breathing hard, dirty, and disheveled, the woman watched the smoke ascend until it met moving air aloft and trailed away. She walked past where the fence had been, up the brick walkway, and into *her* house.

*　　　*　　　*

The white fence had surrounded the farmhouse for nearly 200 years. Family legend said that when that fence—built by William Donaghy in 1749 around the plot where he had yet to build a house for an as yet unknown bride—came down, the family would, too. The fence had survived wind and rain, been unscathed by a fire that destroyed Donaghy's first farmhouse, and been ignored by scavenging troops during the Civil War. Over the generations of its existence, the clean, white fence was the symbol of all the Donaghy's had and others didn't. In the midst of the Depression as houses and fences fell into ruin, only the Donaghy's could afford a groundskeeper whose sole responsibility it was to check the fence's integrity, replace damaged boards, and apply a new coat of bright, white paint every spring and fall. As other farmers lost their lands and homes to the banks and moved into the town to join the breadlines, that fence mocked their passage.

*   *   *

After soaking her aching muscles in a hot bath, the woman looked out the window of her second-floor bedroom. Though the bonfire still burned, she looked past it to the empty holes where the posts had been. Her husband and his family would be angry that the damned fence was gone. They could not understand her need to mark this house that she cleaned, cooked in, and made love to her husband in as her own.

Maeve Donaghy had married well—above her station in life, and she should be grateful they took pity on her, her in-laws said. But life within this family had only absorbed her until little was seen or known of her except the name she took upon her marriage.

*   *   *

Maeve had first seen the fence up close, bright and glaring in the autumn sun, on the day her father took her out of school at 13 to work with him, her mother, and her brothers harvesting others' crops. The intelligent, quiet girl loved animals, loved nursing their injuries, and had an unvoiced dream of becoming a veterinarian; but she never returned to another classroom. After she left school, every day for weeks, Maeve walked by that house and that fence on her way to back-breaking field work. She came to curse the Donaghy girls who peeked through the lace curtains and laughed at her. Warm and smug in the fine, large house, the daughters of that family didn't wear hand-me-downs, didn't get their hands so dirty they wouldn't come clean, didn't walk inside a dirt-floor house and get chicken shit between their toes. The fundamental difference between her and them, Maeve realized, was choice—they had many; she had few. The Donaghy girls chose each day what they wore, where they went, what to do with their day, who to see. Maeve's only choice was to do what others told her to do—first her father, then the man she married.

The white fence's pickets had grinned mockingly at her the day her father had walked her to the front door of the house, barefoot, in a dress made from flour sacks, and pregnant. As her father demanded justice for his daughter from the oldest son of the family, Maeve glanced over her shoulder, out the sitting room window. The fence looked like sharp teeth in a maw that appeared ready to devour her. She wanted to tell her father it was someone else, but before she could Donald Donaghy quietly said, "It's all right. I'll do what's right by her."

Maeve had shuddered as the fence snapped closed on her, shutting her inside the house she would come to hate even more. Prematurely, she felt a quiver behind her navel. Her reprisal—the child not yet real to her—had moved. Months later, when Maeve lay exhausted, sweating, pained, and straining in her childbed, the fence had moved into her room and stabbed her in her contractions. Finally, though, the labor ended, and the midwife forced the "reprisal" into her arms. Maeve looked at the fine, wispy hair and into the trusting eyes and saw the realness of the child. She loved and knew love for the first time.

"James," she said, "Jimmy."

By the time Jimmy was five, the fence enclosed him and three siblings, but Maeve had learned to ignore it. She had to; it took all her strength to endure living in this family. The fence was always there, peripherally, but not as important as cooking meals, cleaning house, minding children, and servicing a husband's physical needs.

*   *   *

Barely four months after the birth of her fourth child, Maeve realized she was pregnant again. She contemplated this while she sat at the vanity in her bedroom. As she stared into the mirror, she realized she was fading. She could look through herself and see the wallpaper on the bedroom walls and the fence through the reflected window. Soon, she'd be completely gone. It was acceptance rather than fear she felt. Gradual dispersion was easy to accept; she was hardly noticed anyway—a nonentity, someone to be referred to not by her name but simply as "Don's wife," another of his possessions.

Maeve tried to will herself back into consistency but couldn't. In this house she was nothing; there was nothing of hers, not even her clothes, as she was constantly reminded, not even her children. She wasn't even allowed to arrange the furniture to her liking.

Maeve got up from the vanity table and crossed to the phone by her bed. The call to the midwife was brief, and they quickly settled on a price. For Maeve any price was reasonable. With a word to the children's nurse, she left the house, walking past the fence to her car. If she looked back she would see it snaking after her, ready to snatch her back. She kept her eyes ahead.

*   *   *

Maeve lay on clean, white sheets spread over the midwife's kitchen table. Did her family eat here, she wondered, after the midwife did her work? Maeve stared at the ceiling, casting her thoughts far away from the tiny kitchen. A twinge in her womb made her flinch. Gently, the midwife patted Maeve's bare thigh. "It's all right," she said. "The pain will only last a moment." Soon, it did ease, and Maeve's hands began to tingle. She held them up before her eyes. They seemed denser now, color and flesh formed and filled their outlines. As the midwife scraped life out of her, Maeve's essence returned.

"I'm done," the midwife said as she folded something in a large towel. Without another word, she left Maeve alone to dress.

As she redressed, Maeve refused to allow any tears, and she watched her flesh grow completely solid again. She left four $20 bills on the makeshift operating table and left for home. When she re-entered the yard and stood by the fence, she looked down at herself and saw she was beginning to fade again. The fence stood more solidly than ever, whiter than ever as it drained her. If she were not free of it, she would disappear, her molecules scattered like smoke on a good breeze. Unmindful of the midwife's admonitions about rest and blood loss, Maeve dropped her purse, kicked off her shoes, and reached for the first picket.

*   *   *

Maeve was ready for her husband's reaction when he returned from a business trip and saw the pile of charcoal and the newly planted flowers blooming from where the fence posts had been. She stood smiling, her new self solid within her, and faced him as a person when he raged into the house. He actually lifted a fist to strike her, but on sight of her and the power emanating from her, he lost resolve and sank into a chair under her incessant smile then grew silent and cold.

Maeve laughed then with a joy so profound it surpassed any physical pleasure she had ever known. The fence was down, and now Maeve moved through the house, her house, always smiling, touching a chair, adjusting the drapes, her hand casual in its caress of ownership. That smile was serene, ephemeral, ubiquitous, and, best of all, would be hateful to her husband and his family. She would smile when she let them into **her** house and when she saw their reaction to what her husband had become—was he fading a bit now? She smiled even broader. She thought, they will fall, they will all fall, and I will live here in my house, on my land.

*   *   *

On Sunday, as usual, the family came for dinner after church. Smiling, Maeve greeted them from where the fence used to be. They accepted the unaccustomed hugs and kisses from her, rendered speechless by her transformation. Her husband sat in a darkened room in his chair and smoked, not responding to their calls of greeting. All day her house abounded with nieces and nephews playing games with her children. Maeve smiled all through dinner even when her mother-in-law complained about the rearranged furniture. She smiled when she overheard whispered gibes from her sisters-in-law about her weight and her clothes. She smiled when her brothers-in-law complained the meat was overdone. After dinner, she smiled when she sent the children out to play in a yard with no fence, free as she was. Let them see, she thought, it was only a fence. Let them see this is all mine now.

She smiled even through the screams.

She was still smiling when her husband carried in a bundle of dirty, bloody rags and laid it on her clean, kitchen table. Her husband shouted for quiet from his relatives. Someone whispered that they would call the doctor. "It's too late for a doctor," her husband said and the house fell silent in finality.

Maeve's husband turned to her with an expression she would see there for the rest of his life—pain and hate and desperation all in a single glance. His eyes drew hers to the thing on the table.

Eyes that had looked up at her in trust upon his birth were open, vacant, flat, filmed like that of a fish too long out of water. Her smile grew into a rictus then dropped from her face.

Maeve had thought the bundle was rags because the clothes she had dressed him in that morning were shredded. Even his face was raw flesh, hanging in tatters. The missing fence which had substantiated her had freed Jimmy to run unimpeded into the gravel road and into the path of a car. The car's fender caught in his clothes, and the car dragged him nearly a quarter mile before the horrified driver could stop.

                        *   *   *

During the wake and funeral, Maeve bore up well, people said. As relatives sobbed around the gravesite, Maeve looked down at herself. If anything, she was more solid, substantial, and real than she'd ever been. The smile returned—small, wan, and mad. As the last clot of red clay dropped on the child's coffin, she pushed all thought and knowledge of him away. She required the same of everyone else. His name would never be spoken in her presence again, could never be used by anyone else in her family for another child. He never existed.

Afterwards whenever Maeve looked out any door, any window, she saw a new fence growing, hard, black iron budding from the holes where her flowers had grown. It took 50 years to grow, but it kept out everything and everyone, except for the little she allowed in.

And Maeve was right. She did outlast them all and died in **her** bed in **her** house on **her** land, surrounded by **her** fence, alone.

What's in a Name?

◆

State Senator Nancy Dale looked at me over her half glasses. "You expect me to read this before the press?" she asked.

"It's the truth," I said.

"The 'truth' of a bunch of convicts."

"Convicts can't tell the truth?"

"Annie, pull in your liberal claws. They will say anything they think will get them out before…"

"…they've paid their debt to society?"

"Exactly."

"Senator, this is a minimum security prison. There are no armed robbers or murderers here. They are bad-check writers and shoplifters."

"Shoplifters are thieves."

"No argument. My Aunt Margery, the quintessential Southern belle, got caught about once a month lifting lace hankies from Newberry's. Do you think she spent any time in the Culpeper County jail? Of course not. Virginia aristocrats don't go to jail. Their fathers pay their shoplifting bills and keep it out of the papers."

The Senator remained quiet, staring at the report in front of her which contained the information that an influential warden at a women's prison was probably running a brothel and had caused the death of a young inmate who wouldn't go along with the scheme.

"Besides," I continued, "the guards' testimony can't be ignored. What would they have to gain by lying?"

She looked at me again. "Annie, I can't take on this issue. I want to run for governor in two years. If I look like I'm coddling criminals, I might as well give up the notion right now."

"Senator, these women have been beaten and raped; one of them was killed, and they sealed the coffin and said it was meningitis."

"So you say." She smiled condescendingly. "Annie, these women are just different from you and me." Meaning they didn't have Virginia pedigrees that went back to Jamestown. "Why, the warden told me some of them are, you know."

"No, what?" I asked, innocently.

"You know," her voice dropped to a whisper, "lesbians."

"Lord, Nancy, this is nearly the 21st century. You don't have to whisper the word, 'lesbian.' The best of families have them. Why do you think Aunt Margery lifted all those lace hankies? They certainly weren't for Uncle Powell."

The Senator stood and came from behind her desk. She took her glasses off and pointed them at me. "I will not read that report at a press conference," she declared. "Write me one that says my investigation could not substantiate the charges."

"I can't."

"You won't."

"Let **me** read it."

"Annie, the only way I'd let you do that is if you didn't work for me anymore." She smiled a pure bitch smile. "But we all know how badly you need a job."

*   *   *

When my male cousins ran the family business into the ground, and I refused to put my regional airline into hock to save their asses, the family name saved them from indictments. No judge wanted to have the Pearce name—a name that had graced the annals of Virginia history for 250 years—stained in that way. Why, that family had contributed so much to the Commonwealth, after all. A few shady business deals could just be ignored, among gentlemen, of course.

Because I was related to the idiots—I wish I could have attributed it to inbreeding, but we didn't have that particular affliction of the gentility—and because of some connection to the family business that to this day I still don't understand (only the lawyers, who made out well on the whole affair, do), the creditors were able to take my business, too.

It made headlines for weeks. My aunts were scandalized because I'd had my name in the papers for something other than being born, debuting, getting married, or dying. Anyway, I found myself with no house, no business, no job, and no money. The only thing I had was that magic name that opened doors which were otherwise locked to all except the privileged. The name had gotten me the job with Senator Dale. Now, that same name got me an appointment with the Governor of the Commonwealth of Virginia.

"You know," he began, as he motioned me to sit in an impressive leather chair across from his equally impressive mahogany desk, "my family is originally from your part of Madison County."

He was telling me he knew that my several times great grandfather had owned his and that he also knew I was coming to ask him for something. If he relished the role reversal, he was enough of a Virginia gentleman not to show it.

But he listened to me; he listened for a long time.

"What can I do?" he asked, finally.

I told him.

He did it.

＊   ＊   ＊

When it was all done, a warden lost her job and went to a prison of the maximum-security variety for manslaughter; the guards who had beaten a young mother to death for not prostituting herself joined the warden there; several judges and state legislators had to resign when their names were found in the warden's client book; and a state senator who had told me to change a damning report lost her bid to be governor. The everyday citizens of Virginia, so disdained by the landed families, love honesty above all, and they do love to see the mighty fall. The governor who had exposed the whole thing went on to become the first African-American U.S. Senator from Virginia. Oh, and I lost my job with the State Senator long before she lost her election.

But I still have my good name; except that my friends and the family I'm still burdened with now call me "Governor Pearce."

Justice

◆

"Your honor," the prosecutor began, "there is only one witness to call for the sentencing portion of these proceedings." The prosecutor turned toward the jury, let her eyes glisten with tears—you could show you were about to cry; you just couldn't go all the way—and softly said, "Kaitlin Haldane."

The bailiff intoned her name in a loud voice and told her she was called to the stand. With a sigh, Kaitlin composed herself, hesitated before she stood, just to collect her thoughts, but it was long enough for the prosecutor's head to whip around and scan the courtroom in search of her. The sympathy was gone from Assistant District Attorney Marcy Hogan's face—thank God the jury couldn't see—and her bright blue eyes icily sought Kaitlin's.

Kaitlin stood, hands smoothing the lay of her business suit. She had removed all her jewelry. Marcy had wanted her to wear them, all the beautiful gold and silver things Mitch had given her. This morning, standing before the mirror, checking her appearance, she had removed them one by one, placing them in a velvet-lined jewelry box, which she then locked and put away in a deep corner of a closet. Marcy had also wanted her to wear no makeup, to appear bereft and weepy. Kaitlin was bereft all right, but she had no more tears. Her make-up was immaculate. Calmly, confidently, she walked up the aisle, through the swinging gate, and back to the witness stand.

"Ms. Haldane," began the judge. Anne turned to him and looked him full in the face. He stopped mid-speech, mouth open, taken back by the serenity there. He clapped his mouth shut, cleared his throat, and began again. "Ms. Haldane, you are not under oath during this proceeding. As you know, the defendant has been found guilty of murder in the first degree, and in the Commonwealth of Virginia, it is up to the jury to recommended sentence, either life in prison without possibility of parole or death by lethal injection. Before the jury arrives at its recommendation, which, by law, I cannot alter, any and all interested parties may address the court and comment on the sentence they deem appropriate. That is, you may tell us what sentence you would like to see the defendant receive. Do you understand?"

"Yes, of course."

Kaitlin turned to Marcy. Peripherally, she could see the jury watching her intently, warm and sympathetic looks on their faces. During the trial when she'd testified, some of them had actually wept. She glanced to the right, toward the defendant's table. The defendant's harried public defender was scribbling notes, planning what he was going to say during summation in stead of listening to the proceedings. Kaitlin stared until the defendant caught her eye. Before he could bring his façade up, she saw his terror. He was scared to death, and, that, she thought was the subtle difference between him and his victim. Mitchell had looked him in the eye before the defendant shot him, and Mitchell had had no fear.

Kaitlin looked back to Marcy and nodded for her to begin.

"Ms. Haldane," Marcy said, softly, solicitously. "I know this is difficult for you, but the jury would like to hear what you have to say about Mr. Roosevelt's sentencing. I'm not going to ask you any questions. I just want you to talk, to tell us what you want." From the pointed look Marcy gave her, Kaitlin realized that Marcy expected her to say only what they had rehearsed yesterday.

Anne turned to look at the 12 faces of the jury—supposedly the defendant's peers. A quick look told her none of them had grown up in The Berg, Alexandria, Virginia's infamous public housing complex, where the defendant had lived most of his life.

"Some of this you've heard before," Kaitlin began, "during the trial, but I want you to remember what's been lost here. Mitchell Sanders helped people. That was all he ever wanted to do. He was the best human being I'd ever known, and never had I been so deeply, so truly, so sincerely loved. We had been together for 11 years, but that all ended abruptly when Mr. Jamal Malcolm Roosevelt shot him in the face." She paused to let the words sink in. The women jurors and a few of the men daubed their eyes again. "He fell on top of me when he was shot. I had his blood and brains all over me." Kaitlin looked at Roosevelt. He was staring at his hands. Show time, Kaitlin decided. "Your honor," she said to the judge, "I'd like to approach Mr. Roosevelt."

The judge was nonplussed. Marcy took a step toward Kaitlin but stopped when Kaitlin held up a preemptory hand.

"Approach him? What on earth for?" the judge asked.

Kaitlin didn't answer, but pursued her additional request. "And I'd like to hold the murder weapon, item of evidence number 14A."

"I object, Your Honor," said the public defender rising to his feet.

Marcy recovered quickly from her surprise. "We are not in proceedings here, Your Honor. Defense not only has no grounds for objection, there is no process for objection."

"Attorneys and Ms. Haldane, side bar, please," the judge said wearily.

The three gathered around the judge, who addressed the prosecutor first. "Ms. Hogan, what do you know about this extraordinary request?"

"She knows nothing about it, Your Honor," Kaitlin replied. "This is my doing. I'm a lawyer, and I've researched this. There is nothing which says I can't approach the defendant and that I can't see the evidence in a sentencing hearing. The evidence is here, because I know Ms. Hogan plans to brandish it during her sentencing summation."

"Look, Kaitlin," Marcy said, "I'm the prosecutor here, and I don't know where this is going, except to unnecessarily prejudice the jury."

"Ms. Hogan, I'm the judge here, and I'll decide where this is going."

The public defender spoke up, "I'm the defendant's counsel here, and since I'm looking for grounds for appeal, I know I have to object to Ms. Haldane's approaching my client. I don't see what her holding the weapon will accomplish."

"I also want to ask him question," Kaitlin said.

"What?" all three of them said at once.

To the public defender, Kaitlin said, "Look, your client has been convicted, but he's going to get to make his own plea for clemency last."

"Prosecution gets the rebuttal," the PD reminded her.

Kaitlin turned to Marcy. "You got your conviction. You did a good job, the prosecution is clean, and there are no grounds for appeal, although I'm sure counsel will try." To them all, she said, "I'm the victim here, remember? The person for whom we wrote all those victims' rights laws. Let me have a little satisfaction."

"Anything else we can do for you?" the judge asked, sarcastically.

Kaitlin smiled. "I promise to recuse myself from any proceedings you're presiding over."

"You just bought yourself a judge." To the PD he said, "Counselor, your objection is overruled. So is yours," he added when Marcy Hogan opened her mouth to speak. "Counsel, return to your tables. Ms. Haldane, back to the witness stand." When everyone was in place, he addressed the court, "The witness may approach the defendant with the murder weapon. Bailiff, please assure, once again, that the weapon has been rendered harmless."

Roosevelt turned to his attorney and was heard to mutter, "What's this? I don't want her talking to me. Ain't she done me enough harm?"

"And how much harm have you done her, you bastard," his attorney whispered back. "You sit there, answer her questions, and keep your cool. We'll get an appeal out of this."

*   *   *

Jamal Malcom Roosevelt stared at the floor. He had tried to say during the trial that he had never wanted to rob the couple walking home from an evening in Old Town Alexandria. The words had failed him when he had wanted to tell the jury how Sweetwater Eddie had told him armed robbery was just an initiation, that if he didn't do it he had no balls, and that if the white folks gave him any lip to teach them a lesson. But Jamal had been totally confused when the man had shown him an empty wallet. He'd spent all his cash on dinner, he said.

"Come on, man. The plastic," Jamal had demanded, waving the nickel-plated .45 at the two. They were both so calm, much more so than he.

"I only brought cash with me," the man had said. "Leave it alone, son."

"You ain't my father," Jamal had snapped back. He'd never known his father, and he didn't like men, especially white men, calling him "son." "All right," he said, "the bitch's purse." Inwardly, he had winced. Momma didn't like that word, and she hated the way his friends bandied it around.

"I didn't bring it," the woman—the same woman now walking toward him—had said.

Jamal hadn't a clue what to do next. Eddie hadn't told him what to do if there was no money.

"What do you need money for?" the woman had asked. "You're not on drugs. Your eyes are too clear. What's it for? Diapers? Food?"

No, no drugs. He'd seen too much of that to fall into that trap, but he'd blurted, "What?" The man was reaching into his inside jacket pocket. Oh Jesus, Jesus, he's got a gun, Jamal thought as he raised his hands to protect his face. He had forgotten the .45 was still in one hand. Jamal wouldn't know until the trial that the man had been reaching for his business card—it was still in his fingers when the body had been bagged—a card for the non-profit organization Sanders ran and where Jamal could get food and other necessities for children. But Jamal had no way to know that at the time. All he knew was his terror at the thought of his mother, who had tried so hard, crying at his funeral and wondering what she had done wrong. Jamal had trembled at that thought, and the gun fired. The man's face puckered as a curtain of stuff fanned out behind his head, showering the woman, who had been standing behind him. The man's body fell on top of her, and she looked dazedly at herself, at the blood and brain matter she was drenched in. She had looked up at Jamal, not realizing he had pissed his pants. Their eyes had met, his stunned and trapped, hers resolved. What had never come out in court was what she had said to him. "Shoot me, too," she had said, "so we can die together." But Jamal had dropped the gun and run away.

Kaitlin stood in front of him, the .45 in her hand; he was her victim now.

*   *   *

"Jamal," Kaitlin said quietly. It took a while before he looked up at her, but he did, eventually. "Jamal, do you love anybody?"

Kaitlin saw the confusion there, then Jamal glanced over his right shoulder. Seated in the first row of the spectator section was Jamal's mother, only 36, holding his two-year old daughter, Jamalia. Kaitlin had indeed done her homework. Jamalia's mother had died of a crack overdose when the child was four months old. Jamal's mother had gotten custody, and it had appeared that Jamal was intent upon being a good father. He just had really bad friends. The Public Defender had insisted upon the girl's presence in the courtroom, one of the few things in his client's favor. The child was adorable, her hair neatly braided and clipped with bright, little bows. Every day when Jamal entered the courtroom, Jamalia had shouted "Daddy!" and reached for him, and Kaitlin could see it tore Jamal's heart not to be able to go to her and pick her up. A deputy had told Kaitlin that Jamal's mother had berated him on her first jailhouse visit.

"How could you have done this to me, boy?" she had demanded, as if all the long hours at her government job had gone for naught. "To be a big man in the 'hood? Well, you're really a big man now, aren't you? Tell me, who is going to be Jamalia's Daddy now?"

Kaitlin saw Jamal's sincerity when he turned back to her and said, "I love my daughter more than anything in the world."

Kaitlin lifted the gun and pointed at Jamalia. Everyone knew it was unloaded and incapable of firing, but instinctively gasps and shouts bounced around the courtroom. Jamalia's grandmother shrieked and tried to get her body between the gun and the child, and that made Jamalia begin to wail. The judge slammed down his gavel and demanded order. Prosecutor Hogan saw the defendant's appeal beginning to take shape, the Public Defender was shouting "Objection!" but with a smile on his face. Kaitlin stood rock solid even when Jamal started to rise from his chair. They looked at each other again, and Kaitlin saw he remembered how Mitch's face had looked when the bullet hit him. He sat back down, tears pouring from his eyes.

"I know," he whispered. "I know. I'm sorry." Kaitlin read his lips more than she heard him over the din. "I never meant for it to happen."

Kaitlin lowered her arm and nodded to Jamal. They understood each other now and both realized her forgiveness. Kaitlin turned and gave the gun back to the startled bailiff before she walked to the rail of the jury box, seeing the red-faced judge in her periphery. The courtroom finally fell silent again, but several of the jury shrank back when she neared them.

"Ladies and gentlemen," Kaitlin said to them, "it seems the easy thing to do to condemn this man to die, doesn't it? Get one more animal off the streets so he won't kill again. How simple and elegant a solution, but what will it do? Will it bring Mitch back? No. Will it bring me sleep at night? No. Mitch will still be dead, and I will still be without him, so what do we gain?

"Don't you think that retribution didn't enter my head? At first I was so angry with Jamal Malcolm Roosevelt that I could easily insert the needle myself, but I remembered something Mitch and I adamantly believed in. No state, no government, has the right to kill. The government is supposed to be the example, and if the government kills, then it's all right for you or me to kill.

"You've heard me called a victim, and I was. I got over it, and I'm moving on with the rest of my life. I can't wallow it that forever, but if you kill Jamal—and you all will have killed him as surely as if you'd wielded the needle yourselves—I'll always be a victim, and so will Jamal, and so will his daughter. And so will you.

"Jamal loves his daughter. Only I saw what was in his eyes when he shot Mitch, and it was fear, not violence, not hate. Today, Jamal got to feel what I felt, and that's all the satisfaction I need. Let him think on what happened every day for the rest of his life in the Greenville Correctional Facility, and let him explain why he's there every time Jamalia comes to visit him. Only then, can we all stop being victims. Thank you, and I apologize if I've upset you. I ask you to remember my one request. Let Jamalia have her father."

Kaitlin Haldane walked from the courtroom, past the glaring prosecutor and shocked spectators. *I kept the faith, Mitchell,* she thought, *although you and Jamal made it hard.*

Five hours later, the jury returned from their deliberations and re-seated themselves.

"Ladies and gentlemen of the jury," the judge intoned, "what say you in this matter? Do you have a recommendation?"

The foreman stood.

"Yes, Your Honor."

PART TWO

◆

My Fantasy World and
Welcome to It

Introduction

◆

I've always wanted to write science fiction, but those attempts never satisfied me—nor the editors of the genre magazines to which I submitted them. Despite my love of the genre and much to my dismay, I'm still not comfortable with science fiction, but I occasionally give it a go. These stories show that I can, at least, give fantasy/science fiction a good try.

Understanding the why of abuse is sometimes less important than moving on. Forgiving the abuser is another matter and involves a lifetime of uninterrupted work. "When Gramma Came to Call" shows to what lengths some people will go to make a point. By the way, "bean si" is the Gaelic spelling of banshee.

"The Last Tuskegee Airman" is a rather dark and troubling story which arose out of the 1994 elections and the rhetoric of Newt Gingrich and his minions. A friend—actually the author of this book's Foreword—said that it was "too angry." I wasn't so much angry as I was afraid of the future that the so-called New Republicans wanted, and I am very happy that most of what I predicted never happened. Events have overtaken Gingrich, but when you look at how he reinterprets history and what he tried to revise in his history "classes," this is an alternate universe we can be happy we avoided—just barely. What the 2000 elections hold remains to be seen, and perhaps there'll be lots of science fiction associated with that!

Medieval churchmen wrote singular treatises on how many angels could dance on the head of a pin. We deem that quaint and amusing today, a wasted pseudo-intellectual exercise. However, in today's cyber-age, you can't help except think that we might be simply lines of codes in somebody's cosmic game. (Bill Gates' perhaps?) I wrote "o:-) (Angel)" four years before the release of the 1999 movie, "The Matrix," which had the benefit of multi-million dollar special effects.

When Gramma Came to Call

◆

My grandmother came to visit today.

That's not particularly momentous unless you know that she's been dead for 20 years.

The doorbell rang, and when I opened the door, there she stood. She wore a pale lavender dress with a neatly folded, matching hankie pinned over her left breast by an amethyst brooch. Her old-fashioned glasses with the rhinestones imbedded in the frames somehow managed to look good on her. Her fingernails were their usual formidable selves, painted bright red to match her lipstick. She looked dressed for church. In fact, this was exactly what she wore when we buried her.

"Hi, Doll," she said, as if this were just a regular Saturday afternoon visit.

I was speechless.

"Are you going to stand there gawking? Come out here right now and give Gramma a hug."

I continued to stand in the doorway, my mouth agape. I really didn't want to "go" where she was, and I wasn't sure I wanted her in the house.

She smiled a familiar smile and spoke in her accustomed Irish brogue, "Oh, no, dear. It really would be unpleasant if I came in there."

I must be dead, I thought.

"No, you're not dead," she said. "I'm just here to talk about a few things, but it looks as if I'm going to be doing all the talking."

I finally managed to find my voice. "Gramma, you have to admit this is a bit, well, unusual."

"Well, of course it is. Dead people don't come to your door every day, do they? Of course not. Margaret Elizabeth, I am not going to stand here on your doorstep for eternity-—which I can do, you know—and wait for you to figure out what's going on." She pointed with one of those exquisite nails to a spot beside her. "Get out here right now."

I could never resist that command tone. I had jumped to do its bidding often enough. When I stepped over the threshold, the yard, the house, the street were gone, and a whirlpool of color disrupted my equilibrium. I reeled with vertigo; then, I felt a firm, living, flesh-warm grip on my arm.

"Don't look down," Gramma said. "You'll get used to it." I must have appeared dubious because she continued, "Goodness, girl, you fly airplanes, and you're going to let a little thing like this upset you."

"Are you here to take me into the light or something?" I asked.

"You're not dead. I already told you that, and I don't want to have to say it again. Now, go ahead and ask the other question."

All right; I'll play. "What are you doing here?"

"I just wanted to drop in and see how you were doing. It's been 20 years, after all."

"Why haven't you been here before?"

"You haven't needed me before."

"And I need you now?"

"Oh, I guess you think you're too grown up to need your old grandmother's help."

"If you've come the way from wherever it is you came from to try the guilt trip, I **am** too grown up for that."

"Fine," she said and turned to walk away from me.

"'Fine?' That's it? 'Fine?' You can't walk away from me like that."

She turned. "And why not?"

"What the fuck is going on here?" I demanded.

"I knew I shouldn't have come. You don't want my help." She unpinned the hankie and dabbed at her eyes. This was a familiar scene, and it had a familiar effect.

"Gramma, I'm sorry. I'm just a bit confused here."

She looked up at me, dry-eyed. "Finally, you've figured it out."

"What? That I'm confused? You said it yourself that dead people don't show up on the doorstep everyday. Of course, I'm confused."

"That's why I'm here," she said.

"You're here because I'm confused, but I'm confused because you're here. This is too complicated."

"Well, life was never meant to be simple, or death, either."

"So, are you, like, in heaven?"

She sighed. "I'm where I'm happy. I wasn't happy until I died. One hell of a note."

"Funny. I always remember you as smiling."

"Through the pain, darling, but you know all about that."

Suddenly, something fearful ran through me.

"Don't be afraid of it," she said, quietly, in the same tone that had soothed nightmares and skinned knees. "There is no *bean si* here. I'm here because you asked for me."

I closed my eyes and hoped when I opened them again, she'd be gone.

"I'm still here, and so are you," she said into my darkness. "You won't hide from this. I won't let you."

I opened my eyes. "What is **that** supposed to mean?"

"You have to deal with the unpleasantness."

My inexplicable fear grew, and my defenses came up. "I've dealt with plenty of unpleasantness."

"No, you push it aside or you find excuses, but you never look unpleasantness in the eye and tell it to go to hell."

"Look, this is enough. I'm scared. Take me home."

"You've always felt you had to survive at any cost. Give in to what you're trying to remember. It can't hurt you."

I stood in a familiar back yard. I looked down at myself. I was a child again, five years old and dressed in a pretty, print dress, lace-edged white socks, and black patent leather shoes. Bruises were fading on my arms and legs.

"Here it comes!" shouted a voice, and I dreaded whom I would see.

My father, a young soldier, had tossed me a brightly colored beach ball, a consolation gift for my being unable to go on vacation with him. He and my mother were separated, and when she learned my father was taking a new girlfriend with him on leave to the beach, she refused to let me go. This was the day he had returned with the present, and we'd tossed the beach ball back and forth for hours. This time, in my confusion over reliving this day, I let the ball smack me in the face and I fell down. My father rushed over to see if I was all right.

"Sorry, honey. Are you okay?"

I looked up into those wise eyes, and I realized that I was 40 years old inside this body. I opened my mouth to tell him not to do what he would do in 25 years—kill himself—but the words that emerged were those of a five-year old.

"I'm okay, Daddy. Is my dress dirty?"

"No, baby."

When I realized I couldn't warn him, my tears came for real.

"Don't cry, honey. You know I have to go." He handed me the beach ball. "Take good care of this, and we'll play the next time I come." He hugged me, and I smelled what I had missed for so long, cigarettes and Old Spice. I watched him walk to his car and drive away.

He was barely out of sight when my mother came out of the house.

"Some gift," she sneered at the ball I clutched to my chest. "Don't think you're going to bring it into the house. You'll break something with it." She reached for it. Although I knew better, I snatched it away. Her face became a familiar mask of rage. She slapped the ball away and grabbed me by the arm. The blows came fast and hard—over in a moment but leaving a lifetime of pain.

When she let me go, I looked around for the ball, but she found it first. Taking a bobby pin from her hair, she jabbed the ball over and over again until there was no hope of repairing it. She threw it in my face. "There! Play with that!"

The next week when my father came, I told him the bruises came from falling out of the swing and that I had "busted the ball."

With a jolt I was back beside my grandmother, but the little girl had come along, too. She looked up at me accusingly.

"I'm sorry," was all I could say.

"Can't you do better than that?" my grandmother asked.

I turned to her, angry myself now. "She was your daughter!" I shouted. "You made her that way!"

"At last!" she shouted in triumph.

"I hated her," I said, my tears real again. "And I loved her. And I only wanted to know why she did that."

"Because I taught her the only lesson I could. Survive at any cost. That was all I, any woman, could do then. Property of my father then the property of the sot he married me to. Each day a battle of wills, but she was the wounded one. All that anger, my anger, her father's anger, all added up and directed at you. Every bruise on you was one on my heart. And I never told anyone."

"We never told anyone because we were trying to survive by being quiet about it."

Gramma nodded. "But no more."

"No more."

How simple it was to face this at last and let it go. Within me was an unbearable weightlessness, threatening to lift me off my feet.

"She loved you, you know," Gramma said.

"I know."

"Now, this circle is broken."

I began to rise, slowly at first, then faster. I looked down. The little girl held my grandmother's hand. They both smiled at me.

"May the road rise to meet you," my grandmother called out, her usual parting to me.

"And may you be in heaven an hour before the devil knows you're dead," I replied.

"I was!"

I ascended, and they receded until they were mere specks. In a wink, they were gone. I kept rising, growing lighter and lighter as I rose.

How will I get down, I thought.

"Why come down at all?" Gramma whispered.

Why, indeed.

I soared.

The Last Tuskegee Airman

◆

The blond, blue-eyed news anchor furrowed his brow, set his jaw, and fixed the camera with a no-nonsense expression.

"Woody Broadwater died of complications from advanced age at the State Mental Hospital today," he said. "Broadwater made quite a name for himself five years ago when he claimed that he and other niggers had flown combat missions 70 years ago in the Great Heroic War, the conflict the defunct United Nations called World War II. Let's go to Daniel Young at State Hospital. Daniel?"

The screen filled with a head and shoulders shot of a crewcut young man whose pancake makeup barely disguised his pimples. It did nothing to cover the tattoo across his forehead, which read, "Berserker." Over his shoulder, just out of focus, was a gray, stone building with barred windows and a crumbling façade.

"Thanks, Roger," he said. "Woody Broadwater was committed to State Hospital in 2010 after he made repeated, unsubstantiated claims that nigger pilots—the so-called Tuskegee Airmen—flew sophisticated airplanes in World War II. In spite of his evangelical persuasiveness among people of diminished intelligence, this network, with the assistance of the Young Historians of Cobb County, debunked his claims, as has been done for other claims of so-called—" His face took on a disdainful expression. "—civil-rights activitists."

File footage of Broadwater from a decade before filled the screen. The aging man was trying to debate a shaven-head, brown-shirted Young Historian who shouted and jabbed an angry finger at the septuagenarian. The reporter provided voice-over.

"This was the scene in Alabama 10 years ago when Broadwater, obviously senile, stood on the steps of the Heflin Courthouse claiming it was the site of the airfield where the Tuskegee Institute had allegedly trained niggers to fly airplanes. The Tuskegee Institute and other discriminatory nigger colleges were closed at the turn of the century as a requirement of the White Race Redemption Act."

The file footage switched to some grainy, fading photographs, and the narration continued.

"Broadwater based his entire argument on faked photos such as these, which had been housed in the old National Air and Space Museum, closed in 2005 after a decade of deterioration caused by the patriotic boycotts of the liberal stronghold for its revisionist stand on the Holy Bombing of Jap Cities.

"Photo experts from the Young Historians were able to show that, as part of a conspiracy by niggers, femnazis, and other subhumans to unseat Christian White Men from their God-given place in society, counterculturalists had taken real pictures of white pilots and superimposed nigger heads on them."

The file footage next showed a courtroom, where a confused Broadwater, his face swollen and bruised, listened as a judge declared him "one crazy nigger" and sentenced him to a mental institution for life.

Young continued, "Broadwater proved to be a contentious patient here at the State Hospital, inciting the crazies that they had rights and privileges that they did not have under the Revised Constitution of 1999. He was disciplined numerous times, including just last week for refusing to take his medication. Broadwater's spurious claims opened a long-healed wound in the White American psyche, a wound caused by agitators and liberals who tried to re-write history and God's laws."

"That's right, Daniel," the anchor interjected. "It boggles the mind how such revisionist ideas got before a God-fearing public, doesn't it?"

"Well, this was before the Controlled Speech Amendment was passed."

"Ah, yes," Roger nodded, "the mend for a lot of ills."

"Yes, it finally put an end to the counterculturalists' claims. The scary part was that these liberals had actually reached into the Holy Sanctuary of the War Department itself and altered records to make it look like niggers had been brave and that they had never lost a bomber they had been assigned to escort."

"Incredible, Daniel," said the anchor, shaking his head. "No wonder the poor old darkie was nuts."

"They were always so easily controlled by the Counterculture for its own traitorous ends. Broadwater attracted quite a lot of attention, but in the face of such unrelenting scrutiny by The Speaker everyone eventually saw the truth."

"The Speaker came out of retirement to head off that affront to history, didn't he?"

Young smiled, his admiration evident, "Well, you can retire the Warhorse, but he still has some kick, Roger."

"That he does. Thanks for that report, Daniel."

Roger turned back to the camera. "Coming up after the break, the State Church adds a tenth Prayer Interval for the schools, sports, and film of the most recent execution of an unwed mother and her bastard."

*   *   *

In the Mississippi National Ghetto, a 12 year old girl, her brown skin scrubbed as clean as her mother could get it with rags and spit, clicked off the antique Sony Watchman to conserve its aging batteries. She pulled open a drawer on a wooden chest and reached inside. Gently, lovingly, she removed a cloth patch, its colors faded, its inscription barely readable. Even though she couldn't read, she knew what it said. Secretly, quietly, her father and grandfather had explained it: 99th Fighter Squadron—Tuskegee Airmen. In Newthistory, such a squadron, such a name, didn't exist, for history had been revised so it didn't conflict with the wave the country began to ride after the elections of 1994, but it was the only history she knew aside from the reminiscences of the two men so briefly in her life.

She reached into the drawer again and drew out a plastic model of an ancient warplane called a Mustang. Its silver paint was chipped and peeled off in places, but its red tail was still discernible, the trademark of the Tuskegee Airmen. Many such planes had streaked the skies over the Mediterranean Sea and southern Europe during World War II, piloted by men who had the same color skin as she. No school would teach this, no one would now admit it on fear of imprisonment, and her mother would get all nervous and weepy if she knew the girl had taken the forbidden toys out in the daylight where someone might see and report her to the Ghetto Police.

Furtively, the girl glanced up at the street-level window. The cardboard had been removed to let in air and light, and through it the girl could see bright blue sky. Sometimes she had even seen a real airplane high in that sky, a tiny speck against the blue. When she did, she would whisper, like a prayer, "Someday I fly a plane, too."

She scrambled atop some piles of broken furniture and boxes until she could lean on the sill of the window. She held the model plane up against the sky. Somehow, its silver paint seemed brighter, the red tail more crimson. The distant planes she saw from that window were silent in their passage, but in her head she knew the plane this model represented must have been loud, shouting its defiance at its enemies— "them mezzershits and fukkers" her grandfather used to say. When he talked about those days, his dead eyes would light up and sparkle, and the girl could always tell the old man was far away in his mind, in another time and place.

The girl began to swoop the model plane back and forth across the square of sky as she made low, growling, engine noises. Using her other hand, she started to dogfight with imaginary enemy planes whose pilots had white skin and blue eyes. It was a game she never grew tired of. In her mind she sat in the Mustang's cockpit, and she moved the controls whose names her grandfather taught her. Yoke, rudder, aileron. Lift, thrust, weight, and drag were her prayers. Pitch, roll, and yaw. Immelman, half Cuban Eight, loop. As the Mustang chased its enemy, the girl's lips puckered around the imitated sounds of long-dead guns and spat out a hellfire of bullets until the enemy plane dived in a plume of smoke and flame and crashed.

And the daughter of the son of the last Tuskegee Airman did a victory roll above the Mississippi National Ghetto and flew where hate would never touch her.

o:-) ("Angel")

◆

The creator-hacker sat at her cosmic computer and mouse-clicked "Interactive."

"Which world?" droned the computer's voice.

"Sol system, third planet," said the creator-hacker.

"That one again?" queried the computer with a mechanical sigh.

"Look, it's my world," said the creator-hacker.

"Yeah, you still keep trying to get it right."

"It was my first creation, all right? I mean, not everybody's first world is perfect."

"Yes, but really! How many wars are we up to, now?"

"Are you going to open the file or not?"

The computer's voice took on an indignant tone. "You're the creator-hacker. You've given me a command. Of course I'll open the file. Do you want to come in at the beginning or after that last string of code you entered?"

"I don't want to relive five billion years. When did I enter the last string?"

"Let's see, about two millennia ago." The computer giggled as it began to review directories and subdirectories in the file. "Oh my. You know that Galilean you had the conversation with the last time you interacted with the character files?"

"Yes?"

"Well, you won't believe what he's told everyone."

*   *   *

The systems engineer regarded the creator-hacker before him. "Generally, when we create worlds, we monitor them more than once in a couple of millennia," he chided her.

"I'd made so many corrections in the code," she said. "I thought this last one would do it."

The engineer was maddeningly patient. "It was certainly innovative to give the physical beings different genders, I must say."

"Well, it was only two, and it was the only way to accomplish replication."

During the silence a galaxy died, several million stars were born, and 4,263 sentient species in the universe became extinct.

"I would think," the engineer said, "that you'd be highly insulted that alfter all the millions of years you've spent on these beings, that they've decided their deity was male."

"Yes, well, I really didn't realize that only two different genders would find so much to disagree about. But a third one just seemed," she shrugged, "superfluous."

Another galaxy came into being, a few million stars died, and 5,728 sentient species crawled out of primordial ooze and walked on dry ground before the systems engineer spoke again.

"This is a real mess. I don't see how we can de-bug this program. I'm for a wipe."

The creator-hacker, whose fractals had been blooming at a calm rate, suddenly flashed vividly. "We can't do that," she pleaded. "There is so much promise. Yes, lines and lines of the program are bad, but some of the subroutines are absolutely magnificent." She slowed her fractal production rate, trying to re-gain control. "Of course, I am biased."

"I agree that many of the subroutines are elegant, but there's no virus-protection. Worms abound throughout. In short, and in the vernacular of one of the subroutines, it's fucked up."

The creator-hacker thought for several millenia before posing her impertinent question. "Did you ever think that a creator-hacker may have created us?" she asked.

"No chance. I've been around long enough to have traced our program through every back door and gateway, around every firewall there is. What's your point?"

"Well, what if we had been created by someone like me, and someone like you hits the delete key?"

A universe was born from a big bang, expanded to its limit, imploded, then exploded again before the systems engineer replied. "If we don't wipe, what do you propose to do about this?"

"Leave it alone?" she suggested.

"Unprecedented." The systems engineer called up his schematic of the Sol System's third planet. He read the program from line 1 to current status. "This is really amateurish in places," he commented.

"It was my first creation," the creator-hacker replied, hoping her fractals didn't reveal the defensiveness she felt.

"But I can understand your attachment to this place, to these heuristic physical creations." His fractals flared sympathetically. "We may not have to wipe this program. They are well on the way to deleting themselves."

The creator-hacker's fractals revealed her embarrassment. "Well, I, uh, placed freedom of choice in the code."

Incredulously, the engineer said, "You trusted a heuristic program with freedom of choice **and** intelligence? Who was your original systems engineer?"

"Uh, you were."

"I was?"

"Yes."

"Hmmm…"

"But I'm entirely responsible, of course."

"No question."

"Look, I'll turn my remaining projects over to other creator-hackers. Let me devote all my time to this."

"No one has ever done that before, either."

"Isn't it about time?"

Millennia went by as pulsebeats. The systems engineeer sent exploratory fractals out to sample the status of the creator-hacker's other programs. All were pristine, exquisite, orderly.

"You do understand that once you embark on this course, you won't be able to create any new worlds?"

"I understand," she replied, but with some sadness. Her unprogrammed ideas for new worlds would never take on life in the cosmic coprocessor. Yet, she began to see how lines of code from those pre-embryonic worlds could be written into her first creation for its improvement. The systems engineer saw the direction her fractals moved.

"That might work," he said, intrigued. Reformatting a hard drive always wiped any programs and files—a difficult choice. The physical beings inhabiting this program were sentient, just beginning to suspect their real origin. A few had even surfed the 'Net to its limit and had seen into the cyberspace of their creator-hacker. They now lived in worlds within their own minds, the pallor of their skin made paler by the light from computer monitors in the dark. Slowly they wasted until cyberspace itself absorbed their electrons, mixed them with starstuff, and shot them to new corners of the universe.

The engineer sighed. This one had always been his best creator-hacker, even if she were unorthodox in her methodology.

"Very well. Turn your projects over to the others and assume responsibility for—what is it called by the way?"

"Earth."

"Where did you come up with that? No, never mind. Just take over 'earth' full time."

"As usual, you are wise."

"I'm the wisest cyberpunk you know."

";-)"

";-)"

The creator-hacker returned to her terminal and began her work on the program for Sol System's third planet. Almost immediately, a military dictatorship released a democracy activist from house arrest without explanation. That was balanced when commandos from a superpower commandeered an environmental organization's boat on its way to stop a mid-ocean nuclear test.

She hacked on, being god and devil, good and evil, life and death. Her fractals glowed and spread with orgasmic satisfaction.

*   *   *

The game ended, and the computer asked the player if he wanted to save the game. The adolescent cybergod smiled. His brilliant gameplay had saved the world yet again. He had received plenty of energy points and a few extra lives to play with. He adjusted his glasses, held together with a cosmic string, and gnawed on a fingernail.

"Yes," he replied.

"Play again?" the computer queried.

"Yes," he said, and his fingers flew over the keyboard.

*   *   *

The creator-hacker sat at her cosmic computer and toggled the key for interactive.

"Which world?" droned the computer's voice.

"Sol system, third planet," said the creator-hacker.

"That one again?" queried the computer with a mechanical sigh.

"Look, it's my world," said the creator-hacker.

"Yeah, you still keep trying to get it right."

PART THREE

◆

Agents of a New World Order

Introduction

◆

Action/adventure is often not a genre associated with women, but I don't like formulaic writing or stereotyping. When many people learn that I write fiction the automatic assumption is that I write romances. Don't get me wrong; I like romance, usually tempered with a healthy sex life and some adversity that makes you appreciate what you have. I do like writing about people caught up in deceptions of their own design. The world of espionage provides me a medium for that. Spies are never wholly machines or wholly human. Their lives when not on a mission resemble yours or mine more so than James Bond's. Theirs is a struggle to do what they need to do, to deal with the mistakes they have made, and to make a better world—though some might question the latter motivation. This unlikely couple you're about to meet have struggled throughout their lives together to be normal, whatever that is, and they find there is always some conspiracy—often of their own making—to keep them in the shadow world in which they've become so comfortable.

I have been an advocate of the United Nations since high school, and I don't mean to imply anything sinister by a depiction of the global, UN espionage network called the United Nations Intelligence Team (UNIT). Rather, the emphasis is on information and shining the light of truth on dictatorship and democracy alike. Ours is a far from perfect world, but it can be a better one. I personally believe that the UN can be a harbinger of that, and, if so, is such a New World Order a bad future?

By the way, UNIT is a fictional organization. Whether or not the UN has its own intelligence-gathering capability is the subject of intense speculation among conspiracy mongers, but none of what I've written should be grist for that mill.

The fall of the Safe Area of Srebrenica in July 1995 was one of the darkest days for UN Peacekeeping Forces. Because of political machinations thousands of miles away, Dutch peacekeepers received no ground or air support and were forced to stand by—a few hundred against thousands of regular Serb army and militias—while the Serbs marched the Muslim men of Srebrenica away. The men weren't found until two years later, in shallow, mass graves. Identification of the recovered remains continues into the present, with the unidentified bodies stored in a natural morgue—the depleted silver mines that once made Srebrenica such desirable real estate. "Giving the Dead Back Their Names" is in honor of thousands, now nameless, who will someday soon be buried with their names, and dedicated to those who are working to see that gets done.

When I taught high school in McLean, Virginia, quite a few of my students had one or both parents who worked for the CIA, located only a few miles away. They had been coached well to give vague answers to the question, "What do your parents do?" I often wondered how the parents explained to their children the need to be circumspect, and I don't think it's coincidence in intelligence organizations, particularly in the National Security Agency, that marriages are formed between employees and children often follow in their parents' footsteps there. "Career Day" poses an interesting dilemma for two people who are comfortable lying but not to someone whose values they are trying to mold.

Ever since I took a graduate level course on The Balkans in college, I have been fascinated by this troubled area of the world. "Blood Vengeance," written in early 1999 before the NATO bombing of Serbia, won Honorable Mention for a Genre Short Story in the 1999 Writer's Digest Contest under the title "Best Served Cold." Many thanks to Stevens Miller whose suggestions made this story better. The pupil became the teacher.

Because of my heritage, the other area of the world which holds my interest is Ireland—the same rifts as in the Balkans, just different religions. "A Father's No Shield For His Child" introduces a character who to me was minor in a story not published here, but William Henry Munro intrigued a friend of mine who suggested he was a character to be fleshed out more. The title is a line from the Seamus Heaney poem, Elegy.

Marriage vows to me have always seemed impossible to keep promises, perhaps why I've dispensed with them in my relationship. Though my two character foils are married, it is an unconventional one, and "For Better or Worse" is a description of the ups and downs any relationship can have. It is mainly a vehicle for the character of Alexei Bukharin, who is a mixture of my father and my own partner, as well as all the other men who have been a positive influence on me. I've managed to find a few.

All right, I gave in and wrote a Y2K story. What can I say; I'm weak. Actually, I thought it would be a good excuse for Mai Fisher to encounter William Munro again, this time with Alexei in the mix. Although "Days of Auld Lang Syne" stands alone, there are several references to events which take place in 1994 and 1995 in my unpublished—I did mention that, didn't I—novel, A Perfect Hatred.

Giving the Dead Back
Their Names

◆

July 1995
The Amsterdam Hilton
Amsterdam, The Netherlands

A check of his watch told Alexei Bukharin that his wife had been in the shower for 45 minutes. Before he could decide whether to go remind her he was in desperate need of a bath, too, from the second bedroom of the suite, his nephew, Kolya, emerged. Clad only in a towel around his middle, Kolya made directly for the room service Alexei had ordered.

Wrinkling his nose as he passed his uncle, Kolya commented, "Dyadya, you still stink." Then, he began to sample the meats and cheeses with abandon. For more than a week he, his uncle, and his aunt had been held hostage by the Serbs at the UN base outside Srebrenica, hostages along with Dutch peacekeepers. MRE's had been their only subsistence. Now that they had been evacuated along with the Dutch to Amsterdam, Kolya wanted to do nothing except eat and sleep for another week.

"My wife is indulging in one of her hour-long showers," Alexei replied.

Kolya stopped pouring a glass of wine and looked up sharply.

"What?" Alexei said, frowning.

"Nothing," Kolya said and finished pouring the wine.

"No," Alexei said, deepening his pitch to a more authoritative tone. "What is it?"

Kolya downed half the glass of wine in one gulp. "It's not vodka, but it will do," he said.

Alexei switched to Russian. "Tell me," he ordered.

"I don't think she should be alone," Kolya replied with a shrug.

Alexei shuddered once and went to the pile of clothing she had discarded. Stiff from sweat and dirt, they were heavy as he picked through them. Her guns were there, both of them, as were the two commando knives she secreted on her person. Puzzled, he turned back to his nephew.

"What happened?" Alexei demanded.

"I wasn't going to tell you."

"But now you are."

Kolya sighed. He had considered what had happened between him and his aunt, and no one else, but his uncle would never be dissuaded from a pursuit for information.

Between ingesting mouthfuls of food, Kolya explained, "That night she and I went out to reconnoiter, we found a group of Chetniks in a farmhouse. They were taunting a 12 year old Muslim girl, and it was pretty obvious that the outcome was going to be a gang rape. We both agreed we needed to stop it, and there were only six of them." Kolya shrugged again, chewing. "We charged in. They fired at us. I shot three, Mai two. One fled. While I sent the girl back to her mama, Mai ran him to ground. When I found them, she was holding his head on her lap, weeping over him. He was no more than 13 or 14, but we couldn't tell that in the heat of the firefight. He was dressed up like a soldier, probably dragged along by an older brother. There was no way to tell that in the dark. He was just another Chetnik being an animal."

Kolya paused, his eyes begging his uncle to let that be the end, but the eyes that were so like his own bored into him, and he relented. He sighed and said, "Totya had shot him in the back then found out he was no more than a child."

"Shit!" Alexei said and headed for the bathroom.

Mai Fisher was a shadow behind the frosted glass of the shower enclosure, but she was moving. Alexei glanced around the bathroom, seeking weapons, razors, anything she could hurt herself with, and found nothing. He decided if intervention was needed, now was the time. Sitting on the closed lid of the toilet, he began to unlace his combat boots and happened to look eye level at the vanity. A round mirror was there, one you might use to apply makeup. Though its surface was mostly clean, Alexei saw some white powder collected in the crevice where the mirror met the chrome frame. The heat of his anger flushed his face red as he wondered if this was her first cocaine use in nearly a decade or if she had been lying to him about it for years.

Alexei stood up and pulled his shirt out of his trousers and stripped it over his head. He unbuckled his belt and let his trousers and underwear fall to the floor, then he stepped out of them before entering the large, marble shower stall.

Mai was in one corner, her back against the marble as the topmost jet from the "shower tower" sprayed her with a strong blast of hot water. Her eyes were closed, her face neutral. One hand held her hair off her face. Alexei stepped into the spray, turning his head right and left to wet his hair. She opened her eyes and stared at him. They were glazed, far away, and her smile was languid.

"What took you so long?" she asked. "I've been waiting for you, thinking it's been a long time since we fucked standing up." Without bothering for his consent, she reached for him, her hands stroking, her mouth on his, as the water cascaded over them.

Alexei took her by the shoulders and pulled her away.

"Where did you get the cocaine?" he asked. At first he thought she was going to protest, then she shrugged in his grasp.

"Most of my teen years were spent partying here in Amsterdam. The drugs may have changed, but the sources are the same," she replied.

"Why?"

"Because I can't look at the faces anymore," she replied. "There are just too many of them. The faces in my head."

Alexei embraced her, holding her head under his chin. The faces in his head, she had long ago helped him dispel, and he was sick with the knowledge he couldn't do the same for her, that only an illegal substance could. When the thousands of dead in Srebrenica would finally be counted, Alexei doubted if there was enough cocaine on earth to push their faces away. He saw the faces, too, but he had always dealt with them easier than she. Had she back-shot the young Serb thinking him to be a soldier or had she wanted to kill a Serb, any Serb, in revenge for what they had done at Srebrenica? As her doubt transformed into guilt, she would see herself no better than the Chetniks in the farmhouse intent upon raping and killing a child.

"You promised me about the cocaine," he murmured.

"I know. I'm sorry. I'm even sorrier that its effects are so temporary."

Angry with himself, he apologized, "This was too soon, all this death too soon after Oklahoma City. I should have said no when we were sent here, but what I said was 'We're ready. No problem.' Fuck this job. We're leaving here and going back to America, and we're taking a year off, maybe the rest of our lives off. I'm not going to lose you to madness. Do you understand me?"

"I'll be all right." Her head tipped back, and her mouth found his again. "I still want to fuck," she murmured against his teeth. Her hips pressed against his groin. "And you do, too, so it seems."

"I don't fuck my wife," Alexei protested, though his physical response was inevitable. "I make love to her."

Before deepening the passionate kiss, she said, "Let's discuss semantics later."

And the killing of children, Alexei thought, giving himself to the time and the need and the woman who was his world.

*   *   *

May 1997
Near Bratunac, Serbia

The tour of the killing field was brief. What interested the forensic scientist more than the place of death were the recovered bodies. Where they died was secondary to why he was here: To identify who they were, to restore the names taken away by death, that was his mission, and he wanted to be about it. He politely but firmly asked through his interpreter to be taken to the tent that had been erected as a temporary morgue. Though the UN worker seemed a bit distracted by the change in plans, he obligingly led the way. The group then side-stepped carefully down a steep hill, slippery from the Spring rains, to a small valley flat enough for the morgue—a large, white tent—to be stable and level. The makeshift morgue was a white slash on the valley floor, 20 meters long, about half that wide, and it was ringed by UN peacekeepers in blue berets and with weapons at the ready.

The forensic scientist was a retired aviation accident investigator, renown for his ability to identify remains in the worst possible condition. With a bit of flesh from an accident site and a DNA sample from a relative to match against, he could at least provide a family with something to bury. Even before DNA sequencing made his job easier, he had pioneered forensic identification and reconstruction techniques for skulls. His work had been revolutionary at the time because often all that could be done was bury unidentifiable remains in a single mass grave after an aviation accident. At first people found it incredible that he didn't need whole bodies, that a scrap of bone could reveal gender, age, medical or injury history to his trained and discerning eyes. Because of his dedication and scientific genius, many a full-sized casket, containing a mere hank of bone or skin, had been lowered into the ground, but a name and a date of death could go on the tombstone. That mattered to families and loved ones left behind. He was optimistic about this job for the UN. Identifying victims of a massacre should be easy compared to the jigsaw puzzle work of aircraft accidents. The likelihood was that he could bring closure to many wretched in their grief, and he was confident as he walked toward the tent that this job would be a good addition to his resume. His pension was adequate, but there was no reason why he shouldn't make the best of his unique talent. He considered just how much he would raise his hourly consultation fee when this contract was finished.

The scientist was impressed when he got closer to the tent and saw the massive, portable air conditioning units pumping cold air into the structure. That meant someone knew what needed to be done to make his work efficient. Closer still, he could feel the cool air leaking from the tent and realized that keeping those units going was costing a pretty penny. That buoyed his optimism. There would be no UN cost-cutting here.

A soldier at the tent's opening—a Finn by the embroidered flag on his uniform—checked everyone's identification and passes, then held the tent flap aside for the group to enter. The scientist didn't react visibly when the smells assailed him from the triangular opening.

Dank, moldy earth, and corruption past the cloyingly sweet stage that he was most familiar with at aircraft accident sites. Behind him he heard a couple of his staff choke at the olfactory assault. Breathing through his mouth, he took out a small jar of Vicks VapoRub and put a generous amount atop his graying moustache, beneath each nostril, before passing the jar around among his staff. The soldier looked at them with an amused expression that said he had been here long enough to become accustomed to the smell.

When the small, blue jar was put back in his hand, the scientist respectfully removed his battered canvas hat and exposed his balding pate to the weak sun. He stepped forward into the tent, walking far enough inside to allow room for the people with him.

"Jesus Christ," he heard one of them mutter.

The tent was lined with row upon row of tables, some manufactured, some makeshift. Sheets of white plastic covered the tables, and atop the plastic were lumps of indistinguishable meat, an occasional skull, a femur, an ulna, a rib protruding from rotting cloth.

"Who is in charge here?" the scientist demanded. He hadn't been told about this. These body parts had been buried for months, perhaps years. From a quick glance he could see mounds of decayed flesh with multiple heads and too many arms, where decomposition had congealed the remains together.

From a corner of the tent a woman walked forward, a white lab coat over black BDU's. Her hands were inside latex gloves, and a surgical mask covered the lower half of her face. Except for two white streaks at her temples, her hair was dark, as were her eyes, and when she spoke, it was with a cultured English accent.

"I suppose I am," she said. "I'm Mai Fisher from the UN Security Forces. You must be Dr. Clifton Hume." Her latex gloves were contaminated, and she didn't extend a hand to shake.

"Yes, I am. This," he said, waving a hand toward the remains barely recognizable as human, "is not what I expected."

The woman pulled her mask down to reveal her face. Late 30's. Good skin. Celtic bone structure, the forensic scientist in him noted.

"This is Bosnia, Doctor. What **did** you expect?" she asked.

Hume was unaccustomed to such sarcasm. "How long have these people been in the ground?" he demanded.

"Two years."

Behind him, his staff muttered in disbelief, though Hume was beginning to realize the challenge being placed before him.

"Any idea how many?" Hume asked.

"Anywhere from 5,000 to 7,000," was the reply. "Closer to 7,000."

"Oh, my God," someone said.

"The vast majority are Bosnian Muslim males," Fisher continued, "between the ages of 16 and 60. They were shot at four to five different locations in and around the safe area of Srebrenica in July of 1995. The bodies were bulldozed into mass graves. This is one site of three we know of. There are likely others we haven't found yet. We have a list of names of missing men compiled by the women who survived, along with identifying information. Occasionally, we get lucky and find a wallet or an identification card, but that's rare. They were all robbed before they were murdered."

"This could take years," said Hume, pensively, his scientific curiosity building.

"My understanding was that you were retired. You have all the time in the world. The UN War Crimes Tribunal has the funds to support this effort, and your contract will be extended as necessary."

Hume looked around again. As both a scientist and a humanist the appeal of this project was tempting: to put families at ease, give them something to bury in a place where they could mourn. But the extent of the job could overwhelm. **Seven thousand** lives ended, their mortal remains scraped along the earth like so much unwanted debris.

"Why did this happen?" he asked Mai Fisher, then felt somewhat foolish, believing he'd asked an unanswerable question.

"Who knows?" she replied, shrugging. "Maybe the fathers and grandfathers of these men were in the Utashi in World War II and killed Chetniks, and the Chetniks' descendants finally got revenge. Maybe it goes back to 1689 and the battle of Kosovo. Maybe it was simply madmen out of control, or young soldiers with a blood lust to settle ancient scores. No one knows why. No one cares. After all, this is only Bosnia."

Hume considered her words. The deadly quiet in the tent lured him to watch as a few UN workers moved about, making notes by clumps of remains, reverently covering them or gently moving them to a work table for closer examination. What lay before him was an opportunity of a lifetime. In his years of forensic identification at aircraft accidents all over the world, he had perhaps identified two or three thousand bodies. In one place he could double that number. The scope would be staggering even for a young man, and he was not that any more.

However, the stark humanity of this place and the burden borne by the young woman before him was compelling.

"We've arranged for shelter for you and your staff a couple of miles away at the UN compound," said Fisher into his reverie. "The prefabs are a bit more crude than the usual hotel but more comfortable than any hotel around here, and every four days you'll get three off. There'll be transports to Zagreb, Vienna, or Rome." Her tone indicated that Hume's staying was a *fait accompli*.

"You seem certain that I'll take this on," Hume replied, hoping he was hiding his eagerness to get started.

"Aren't you?" she asked, a slight smile on her lips. "If you don't, then the take on you was all wrong."

"The 'take' on me?"

"Your former colleagues at the FAA assured me you particularly enjoyed challenges."

"Challenges, yes. Impossibilities?" Hume looked around again and shrugged, but his expression told the woman and his staff that he wouldn't be walking away. The challenge had been accepted.

"Are you certain," he asked, quietly, "of the possible number of victims?" She nodded. Still dubious, he explained, "Sometimes relatives exaggerate. Sometimes they try to defraud. One plane crash I did in Africa, the government offered $300 per victim to the families. If all the families who came forward claiming a relative on board had one on board, there would have been about a thousand people on that 737."

"This was a military operation," Fisher replied.

"Sometimes militaries, as we well know in America, up the body count for propaganda effect."

"This military, if anything, down-played the body count, Dr. Hume. The range I gave is accurate. It has been verified independently, and, if anything, it will go up."

"How can you be so certain of that?"

For a moment Hume thought she might not answer, then he was startled by the expression on her face. His question had triggered the remembrance of some horror she had buried, likely at the same time these bodies had been hastily interred. When she answered him, he had to strain to hear her whispered words, and when he understood them, he was thoroughly convinced to stay.

She said, "I was there."

*   *   *

May 1997
UN Compound
Bratunac, Serbia

Sometimes Mai Fisher felt like Lady MacBeth bemoaning the spots of blood that only she could see on her hands and which never went away even after constant washing. When she doffed the white coat and pulled off the filthy latex gloves at the end of each day, she still felt as if the stench and mess of death had been tattooed into her skin. She wished emotions could be as easily discarded as latex gloves and lab coats, sent away for biological waste disposal. No, emotions followed her everywhere, into her off hours, into her sleep, what there was of that. Perhaps now that Dr. Clifton Hume were here, she could leave, distance would lessen her guilt, and there would be sleep. Maybe the faceless shapes that haunted her dreams would go back into their hell and wait until this cruel land called her back. And it would. It had so often since 1992. She continually returned to the Balkans because, unable to stop massacres, she did her penance by surrounding herself with the remains of the victims. She had selected her atonement by starting the identification of the dead of Srebrenica, and though her personal attempts had been feeble, she had sought and received the assignment to select a consultant to do the job properly. When Hume's name came up on a list of possibilities, she had studied his impressive resume and read his scientific papers. When she read how he likened forensic identification to restoring the lost names of the dead, she knew she had the right man. He would succeed, and the women of Srebrenica would have a place to go and mourn.

The men of Srebrenica would have their names back, but their souls would forever be restless in Mai's conscience.

Twenty years ago in the midst of the Cold War, she had become a spy, a legacy from her parents. The Cold War had been black and white, good and evil, the two sides so easily defined. Its aftermath was a gray area where friends became enemies and enemies friends, and her long-established espionage philosophy was seldom sufficient for current situations. Success had been easy in the Cold War, and failure was too common in its passing. Her adjustment had been difficult because the profession she had taken such pride in had passed her by. Her ideals were outmoded, her optimism naïve. Though her skills were still unsurpassed, the world of hands-on spying was disintegrating into ubiquitous privacy-intruding cameras, leaving such as she to the realm of industrial espionage, providing personal security for hire, or, heaven forbid, the profession of private detective or fugitive recovery. The Balkans. Africa. The Middle East. China. Korea. India. Pakistan. Northern Ireland. So many global hot spots, so few human spies. Who needed to risk lives when you had satellites in orbit that could read the headlines of newspapers over your shoulder or listening devices that picked up conversations from their vibrations against windows?

And she was growing tired of the game, the biggest shock of all. She had never envisioned a day where the risk and danger would no longer lure her, but that day was approaching.

Hume had asked how she could be so certain of the number of victims the Serbs had bulldozed into mass graves around Srebrenica, and she had answered that she'd been there. Seen most of it. Able to stop none of it.

Mai shook her head. When those thoughts came into her mind, the butt of her gun fit too neatly into her palm, pressed too quickly against her temple. She was one person. One person cannot stop an army bent on destroying an ethnic enemy, as she well knew. She was half-Irish, after all.

No, she could be at peace tonight, knowing that Dr. Hume's work would lay all her ghosts of Srebrenica to rest and return to the dead their names.

Except for the constant companion of her waking and sleeping hours—one boy, playing soldier, who now lay alone and forever unnamed in a grave no one would ever find.

Career Day

◆

Natalia Burke waited patiently in the kitchen for her grandparents to emerge from their office. They would know that she was home from school because it was the usual time and because the house's elaborate security system would have heralded her arrival. She poured herself a glass of juice and sat at the counter where she could see the door to the home office. Two lights on the entry keypad glowed green and red, which meant that they were in the office and the door was locked, respectively, and that meant they were inaccessible.

That had always been the cardinal rule. She was never to go into the office unless one or the other of them was with her, and she was never to knock on the door while that particular red light was on unless it was an emergency—"a life and death emergency not an I-need-a-new-dress emergency" had been her step-grandmother's definition. There had been a superseded cardinal rule that had been more prevalent when Natalia was younger—always knock on the grandparents' closed bedroom door before entering. That rule had been put in place when she was eight and came to live with them. One night after a particularly bad nightmare, she had sought their solace. So she'd seen them in the middle of having sex. She had been eight, after all, and was well aware what adults did behind closed doors. Then, she thought it completely gross and couldn't see why adults wanted to go through all the fuss. When she'd coyly asked why she had to knock first—mainly to see her step-grandmother's reaction—her step-grandmother had explained using a great many large, polysyllabic words which Natalia knew boiled down to "Don't come in because we're having sex." Natalia sighed lightly. She was 16 years old now and really had no reason to knock on the closed bedroom door anymore.

Of course, the closed and locked office door didn't necessarily mean the two of them were working. It could mean that they started out working but ended up having sex. Her grandparents had sex a lot, at any time of the day or night and under any circumstances. You didn't live with them without realizing that. Natalia didn't know exactly why that irked her. She actually thought it was pretty amazing that her grandparents wanted to do the wild thing so much, other than her step-grandmother was much younger than her grandfather and he was a bit insecure about that. Natalia supposed that when he was 35 and her step-grandmother was 20, he probably had other things on his mind than now when he was nearly 60 and joked with his wife about trophy husbands.

Marrying a much younger person for a second go-round seemed to be a family tradition. Her new stepmother was also a great deal younger than her father. Personally, she thought that boded well for when she was in her 40's and could expect to marry a man in his 20's. Her step-grandmother would find that amusing, her grandfather would give her that stern look that said, "You're too young to be thinking about such things," her stepmother would just smile nervously and wonder if it were some plot against her, and her father, well, he would just freak.

When her grandparents didn't emerge right away, Natalia knew she was right about what was going on behind the closed door. That annoyed her for no reason other than her grandparents, her legal guardians, had sex constantly but indicated to her that she wasn't old enough to indulge. Normally, she would have accepted their wisdom— they **were** particularly wise, and cool, too, but she would never let them know she thought that. Recently, though, one particular boy at school was looking pretty good, and Natalia's daydreams were full of thoughts of naked bodies pressed together and orgasms. She smiled slightly. What would her step-grandmother do if Natalia were to ask, "Mummy, what does an orgasm feel like?"

Since that wasn't the subject she wanted to discuss with them this afternoon, Natalia decided to file that away for just the right situation. She rarely saw her step-grandmother nonplussed, but Natalia had also learned quickly that she was the only person who could discomfit the woman. Being a teenager sucked sometimes, most of the time, really, but there were those rare moments of triumph when you just knew you'd put one over on the adults and there was little they could do about it.

Okay, she thought, they know I want to talk, so they're being deliberately inaccessible.

Then, the two lights on the keypad switched colors, indicating the door was no longer locked and the occupants were emerging. And so they did, amid her step-grandmother's throaty laughter and her grandfather's bemused murmuring. Their faces were flushed, and her step-grandmother's hair was just a bit mussed. Christ, they **had** been at it again. Sometimes Natalia thought they just waited for her to be out of the house so they could fornicate on every piece of furniture.

"Hello, Mummy, Papa," Natalia greeted, putting a bright smile on her face.

"Hello, Terror," her step-grandmother said, using the nickname she thought uproarious.

"How was school?" her grandfather asked.

"The same as it was yesterday," Natalia replied.

"Was yesterday boring or unfulfilling? I can't remember which," said her grandfather.

Natalia rolled her eyes in that quintessential adolescent gesture. Actually, she adored her grandfather. He was tall and handsome for an old guy. He wore his hair long for an old guy, too, and it was nearly all gray, but it was completely cool. He had always been fun to be with and comforting when that was needed. From him she had learned a variety of things unusual for most girls her age—among them how to build decks and drywall rooms, how to navigate both a motorboat and a sailboat. She could rely on him, which was certainly more than she could say for her own father, who had dumped her on her grandparents when Natalia was eight.

Unfair to Daddy, she told herself. Her own mother had just been killed in the same car accident where her father had been badly injured. Natalia, because she was belted in the back seat of the Volvo, hadn't had so much as a scratch. She supposed her father had found that difficult to deal with. Her grandfather had taken her into his home with no questions asked, and she had had a pretty decent adjustment. She loved her step-grandmother, too, a bit more understanding of her needs but with a whole boatload of expectations. Theirs was sometimes the uneasy relationship that mothers and daughters experienced in the daughter's adolescent years. Even when Mummy was right, Natalia just felt compelled to be rebellious. And Mummy was practically omniscient. There were rarely any secrets Natalia could call her own. Mummy wasn't a snoop. She could just look at you, and you spilled your guts.

Like now. She was studying Natalia with a practiced eye.

"What's up at school?" she asked Natalia.

"Oh, it's nothing, really," Natalia said, with a long-suffering sigh. If she milked this sympathy thing a little she might get an hour added to her weekend curfew. That tone of voice brought skepticism from her step-grandmother, concern from her grandfather, so she directed her next words to him.

"We have this, like, totally stupid, bogus assignment," she said. "And I just, like, am going to blow it off."

"What is it?" he asked.

"I told you. It's really stupid. It's not important enough to bother with."

"Obviously it is," her step-grandmother said, "or you wouldn't have brought it up." She had poured herself a glass of cranberry juice and now leaned on the counter across from Natalia.

I really, really hate it when she's right, Natalia thought, which is, like, all the time.

"It's stupid, and, besides, I can't do it anyway," Natalia said with a rather dramatic sigh.

"You can do anything you put your mind to," her grandfather said.

"It's not that I'm not capable of doing it. It's, like, I can't." The two of them stared at her, unasked questions on their faces. "Okay, well, we're having, like, this stupid career day at school in a couple of weeks, and all of us were supposed to write down what our parents do, and so, I, like, wrote that my father was an astronomer in Hawaii, and the stupid teacher goes, like, 'Well, Natalia, your father isn't here to be a guest at career day, so write about what your grandparents do.'" She stopped. That was explanation enough. The two of them stared back at her. She was expecting panic but got nothing, just—blandness.

"And what did you tell her we did?" her grandfather asked.

"That you worked for the United Nations, which was, like, totally not good because then, like, she wanted to know all about it, and I, of course, had to say, like, 'I don't know,' because I don't know, and she's, like, 'You don't know what they do?' and I'm, like, 'No, I don't,' and she goes, 'You have to know something,' and I go, 'Like, no, I don't.'" She paused for a breath.

"Amazing," her step-grandmother said, "that was one entire sentence. Thank God you write more articulately than you speak."

"What's the bottom line?" her grandfather said. He was always like that, straight to the point, whereas her step-grandmother liked to let you twist in the wind a bit.

"I tried to tell her you two were too busy to come to a career day, and she said, 'Lots of parents are busy, but they make time for something as important as this, so have your grandparents call me.'"

"All right," her grandfather said, "we will call her and extend our regrets. Which teacher is it?"

Natalia didn't answer right away but stared at her grandparents. She summoned her resolve.

"What exactly do you do, anyway?" she asked, hoping she sounded casual.

They didn't exchange a look but continued to stare impassively at her.

"We work for the United Nations," her grandfather said.

"Duh, Papa," Natalia replied. "So do, like, what, thousands of other people? What do **you** do?"

This time the two of them did exchange a look, one that she had often seen them exchange and which spoke silent volumes between them.

"You had to know I was going to ask that someday," Natalia continued. "I mean, all these strange people come and go, like Uncle Snake, and my cousin Kolya with that skull tattoo, and Olga, my 'au pair' who acts like everyone who comes near me is going to kidnap me, and the two of you go away for days and weeks at a time and never say where you're going. I think you're, like…"

"Like what?" her step-grandmother said.

"I don't know. The Mafia or something."

"No," her grandfather said, "we're not in the Mafia, American, Italian, or Russian. We advise governments on security issues, and, as such, our work is classified, so we will be unable to participate in your career day."

She hated it sometimes when he was right, too.

"I mean, like, couldn't Mummy come and talk about her businesses or something. You said it was totally cool for me to talk about how I worked for Euro Enterprises over the summer and went to Bosnia."

"How important is this to you?" her step-grandmother asked.

"Well, I'm, like, the only one whose parents, or steps, or anything won't be participating. I mean, if you send Roisin, it wouldn't be the same."

"Why would I send Roisin?"

"Well, she's, like, the COO, you said, the Chief Operating Officer."

"And I'm, like, the CEO, the Chief Executive Officer," her step-grandmother mimicked.

"As long as you don't decide you need a trophy husband," her husband interjected.

"Can a trophy wife have a trophy husband?" she asked him.

Natalia sighed. They could joke at the bloody stupidest times.

"Well?" she prompted.

"I'll be happy to do that."

Natalia was pleased, but there were still so many unanswered questions.

"Why do I think this conversation is not over?" her step-grandmother said.

"I really would like to know what exactly it is that you do," said Natalia. "Like why my grandfather nearly got killed that time, like why I came into the bathroom once and found you bleeding, Mummy, like why I see bruises and cuts on you both sometimes, like why…"

"I think we get the picture," said her grandfather.

For a second, Natalia thought her grandfather was angry, but she realized his expression was one of regret.

"It's not really something we can discuss with you, for your safety," he said. "It's why we prefer to keep a low profile and why we have Olga to make certain you stay safe. Let's just say that there are people out in the world who do not abide by the laws of their countries or the regulations of the UN, which they swore to do, and we make certain their governments know about their actions. Sometimes, when we do that, those people are not happy with us, and they try to stop us from turning them in."

After a moment, Natalia nodded. "So, you're, like, spies," she said.

"Why would you think that?" her step-grandmother asked.

Natalia sighed. Sometimes they equated youth with being totally dense. "Well, for starters, my Dad once said that Papa and Uncle Snake stole him out of Russia, so, I figured that was not exactly a normal thing for someone to do. Then, there's Olga who knows all of these really weird things…"

"I doubt very seriously that Olga has discussed 'weird things' with you," her step-grandmother said.

"No, but, sometimes, she says things like, 'Little One, if you see same car follow you more than three turns, call on cell phone.'" Natalia's imitation of Olga's thick, Russian accent was flawless. "So, I mean, how does she know things like that?"

"I think you've been watching too many movies," her grandfather said.

"Okay, look, I can see this makes you guys uncomfortable, just don't treat me as if I'm stupid. It's not because I watch too much TV or too many movies. It's because fucking weird things go on here."

Her grandfather looked at his wife, not accusatory but a bit exasperated. "It's because of you that she so fluidly interjects the word 'fucking' into her speech," he said.

"Why would I think she listens to that when she doesn't listen to anything else I say?" his wife replied.

"We're not getting side-tracked," Natalia said, "into one of your little joke fests. I'm right, aren't I?"

"And what if you were?" her step-grandmother said. "Do you think that means we could come to your career day and talk about it?"

"Oh, please," Natalia said. "That's not the point."

"What is?"

"I would just like to know the truth."

"Do you think we've lied to you?" her grandfather asked, his face all serious.

"Well, no, not exactly lied. Sort of like the way the President answered his grand jury questions. You know, 'depends on what the definition of is, is?'"

Her grandfather seemed taken back by the comparison. "I hardly think you can compare my integrity to his," he said.

"Well, you have the same color hair," his granddaughter replied. And, it was on her lips to say, you used to do the same thing to Mummy he did to his wife, but she thought that best not to bring up. Her grandfather's expression was wounded, and she was immediately regretful. He turned to his wife.

"Some help would be appreciated," he said.

"Your hair is the same color but much nicer," she replied.

"Guys," said Natalia.

Her step-grandmother's gaze was far less forgiving. "If you think we have lied to you, I'd like to hear some specifics," she said.

Of course, she would ask that. How did you quantify your feelings and impressions about things?

"Well," Natalia said, "you always say you're 'away on business.'"

"When we're away, we are on business," said her step-grandmother.

"Then, there's Uncle Snake," Natalia said. "I mean, how many people have a one-armed honorary uncle named Snake who sees people stalking him behind every bush and shrub?"

"And?"

"He said he used to be with the CIA."

"A lot of people work for the CIA. Not all of them are spies."

"He carries a gun."

"A lot of people carry guns."

"So do you."

"We own guns…"

"You wear one," Natalia said. "All the time."

"All right," her step-grandmother conceded, "we wear the guns we own. Papa explained about people being upset with us because we turn them into their governments for crimes."

"How do you prove these people have committed crimes against their governments?"

"We catch them doing it."

"How do you do that?"

This time her step-grandmother looked to her grandfather.

"I could use some help myself," she said.

"Your hair looks nothing like the President's," he replied.

Her expression was scathing for him, but mollified when she turned back to Natalia.

"If we have lied to you about anything, it was to protect you," she said. "I understand that you may not be able to rationalize that dishonesty can protect you, but you'll just have to take our word for it."

"That time I found you bleeding in the bathroom," Natalia said to her step-grandmother, "what happened to you? And not 'I had an accident,' which is what you told me then."

"This conversation is over," said her grandfather, a sudden anger in his voice.

"Papa…"

"No, it's over. Mummy has agreed to come to career day in her capacity as CEO of her company. There will be no more talk about spies. Am I clear?"

Natalia's own temper, heralded by her shock of bright, red hair, flared. "Fine," she announced, getting up. "I guess if I'm that untrustworthy, I'll just go to my room."

"Guilt trips don't work," her grandfather said.

"Well, then, I'll just accept that you both have been lying to me, like, my entire fucking life."

She walked away and made sure they could hear every tread she stepped on all the way up the stairs to her room.

*   *   *

Mai Fisher turned to her husband and said, "Oh, yes, the Neanderthal approach really works."

"What else could I do?" responded Alexei Bukharin. "Tell her that we're spies?"

"I think she's figured that out."

"Surely you didn't want to answer her questions, because if you told her you'd been shot that time, you know what the inevitable next question would be."

"Yes," she said, soberly. "She'd want to know if either one of us had ever shot anyone."

"Exactly why I opted for the Neanderthal approach."

"We're well past where she accepts the first thing we say to her. She's a smart young woman, and she's quite capable of seeing through the subterfuge."

"A subterfuge, which, for spies, we haven't been very good at maintaining."

"Obviously, and, also obviously, Olga hasn't been as circumspect as we hoped."

"She might think she's still recruiting for the KGB," he replied, smiling. He instantly saw that his wife wasn't amused. "She's probably only taught the girl things that will help her personal security."

Mai was thoughtful for a moment, and Alexei knew better than anyone that could be particularly uncomfortable.

"You know," Mai said, "if we tell Natalia she can't talk about this to anyone, she'll not gossip."

"I'm certain of that," he agreed then sighed. "The older she gets, the likelihood that she picks up some of this on her own is high, meaning that the risk of her becoming a target grows as well. And Olga isn't getting any younger. In fact, she's three years older than I."

"I didn't notice your age about a half hour ago."

"Attributable in large part to your skill."

"Yes, well, that aside, she's not going to let this be."

His face set in a stony inflexibility she easily recognized.

"We are not telling my granddaughter anything about what we really do," he declared. Turning abruptly on his heel, he walked back into the office and locked himself in.

Natalia could be excused for walking off in a huff, that being expected of an adolescent. The same behavior on a supposedly mature man in his 50's was not expected. So, which to deal with first? She drained her cranberry juice, wishing it were red wine, and headed upstairs.

"I'm e-mailing," came the muffled reply to Mai's knock on the door. Mai rapped a bit harder this time and could practically hear the pained sigh from the other side of the door. The door opened, and Natalia blocked the doorway.

"May I come in?" Mai asked.

"If I say no, you'll just remind me it's your house," was the reply.

"That's a bit uncalled for," Mai said.

"I don't want you to come in if you're just going to tell me more lies."

"Even more uncalled for."

"Well, I don't want to be lied to."

"I'm not going to lie to you."

Natalia narrowed her eyes. "If you're what I think you are, you could lie to me and I'd never know it."

"Probably, but I'm not going to lie to you."

Natalia glanced over Mai's shoulder. "You're up here alone," she said, "which means that Papa doesn't agree with what you're going to say."

"Papa doesn't know I'm up here."

The girl was thoughtful for several moments, then she stepped back, letting Mai enter. Natalia went over to her computer and logged off as Mai closed the door, walked into the room, and sat on the bed. She gave a cursory glance at the chaos around her, thought about chiding, and decided not to.

Natalia spun in her desk chair so that she faced Mai, folded her arms over her chest, and said, "All right, I'm listening."

"That time you found me bleeding in the bathroom," Mai began, "that was because someone shot me."

Natalia's eyes widened. "Shot you? Like, with a gun?"

"Well, it certainly wasn't a pea-shooter."

"Wh-why?"

"Because I recognized him, and he recognized me and knew that I recognized him, and he didn't want anyone to know where he was or what he was up to. So he shot me."

"Did he… Did the police catch him?"

Mai carefully phrased her reply. "Yes, the police took him away." In a body bag, she added mentally, where I put him. "The time that Papa was hurt and you came to hospital in Oklahoma City," she continued. "We were there because we were trying to stop the man who did it."

"You know that guy?" she asked, shocked.

"Yes, but I can't tell you much about it. That's the truth."

"How did you know he was going to blow up that building?"

"I made friends with him, you see, without telling him who I really was, and because we were friends, he told me things."

"But you couldn't stop him."

A wave of memories and disappointment washed over her. "No, I couldn't. I tried very hard, but sometimes the things you believe in, right or wrong, are more important to you than friendship." Or infatuation, she thought. She watched as Natalia's discomfort with the knowledge she thought she wanted grew.

"I don't think I want you to tell me anymore," Natalia murmured.

"A bit late for that," Mai snapped. "You started this, and I've never allowed you to back out on anything you've started."

"I'm afraid…" Natalia began then stopped. She gnawed her lower lip.

"You're afraid that your Papa and I are going to turn out to be people totally different from whom you've known all your life?" Natalia nodded. "Well, we're not. We're the same as we've always been to you. We try to stop bad people from doing bad things. We love you as we always have from the moment you were born, and that will never change, no matter what we do in our work."

"Why did you pick this kind of 'work' to do?"

"So the world would be safer, more peaceful, a better place. Sounds a bit trite, but that pretty much sums it up." The two stared at each other a bit, and Mai had a slight concern. The girl was as manipulative as any teenager could be, and Mai could envision this knowledge being held over her and Alexei's heads at the next adolescent uprising. "Now, I've trusted you with this for the very reason I knew I could trust you," Mai said. She wasn't above being manipulative herself. It was bread and butter in her profession. "You have to understand how important it is that this remains between you and me. You're smart enough to figure out why."

Natalia nodded but didn't speak.

"And Papa will just be upset if he knew we talked about this. I'm not asking you to deceive him, because I know you would never do that. If you think about this for a while and decide you have other questions, I'll be happy to try to answer them for you. Deal?"

"Deal," Natalia replied, softly.

"All right, then, when's this career day?"

"Next Wednesday at 10."

"I'll be there." She smiled at Natalia. "I'll even come in a limo if you think it'll put the point across."

"God, no! That would be so totally embarrassing." She was thoughtful again. "But you will talk about your airplane, won't you?"

"I will. Would it be less embarrassing if I had the pilots do a flyover?"

The girl's eyes fairly gleamed with that, and Mai was amused by what did and didn't embarrass a teenager.

"Well, then, I hope that my willingness to confide in you was helpful," Mai said. "You hurt Papa's feelings when you accused us of lying to you."

"I know. I'm sorry." The contrition was real. "And, uh, thanks, Mummy. I guess."

Mai smiled and stood up, looking down into a face that was a woman's, not a girl's anymore. How much had the knowledge she just received contributed to that transformation? She brushed Natalia's cheek fondly with her fingertips and turned to go.

When she reached the doorway, Natalia called to her. "Mummy?"
Mai turned, her hand on the doorknob.

"I have one more question," Natalia said, "then I won't ask any more."

Mai waited, watching Natalia form the question in her head, almost hearing it in her own before the girl spoke.

"Mummy, have you or Papa ever killed anyone?"

Knowing full well it would answer her question, Mai said nothing and closed the door, shutting Natalia away with the terrible knowledge she had sought.

*   *   *

In their office Alexei was seated on one of the sofas that faced the French doors. Beyond was the large expanse of yard that stretched down to the Potomac River. At this point more than a mile wide, it rushed past, swollen with early fall rains, to meet up with the Chesapeake Bay some miles away. Alexei was drinking a brandy, a bit early in the day for that, but Mai understood. Right now, one wouldn't taste so bad. Natalia had been correct: This day had been inevitable, but that didn't mean that it had been easy to sit with a young girl whose values you were trying to mold and tell her you sometimes did sneaky things in the name of good. When Mai was barely older than Natalia, she had chosen this life, and she had questioned that decision every day since. However, like the value of commitment she was trying to teach Natalia, she had never wavered in her duty.

Quietly she crossed the room and sat beside Alexei, not touching him, to share the view. For nearly a quarter hour they sat that way, their thoughts for company. Finally, it was Alexei who spoke.

"You told her," was all he said.

There was no emotion to his voice, and that bothered Mai. When he retreated into that place where he used to be the person whom everyone called the Ice Man, anger was preferable. Anger meant that you were capable of feeling. The Ice Man had been known for his lack of that human attribute.

"Not all. Enough for her to understand," she replied. "She also understands the need to be prudent."

"I forbade it, but you did it anyway."

After all these years, why does that surprise you, she thought. "I had to do what I thought was best for her," Mai replied. When he didn't reply, she added, "She was right. We knew this day was coming. We just operated in a state of denial, foolishly thinking our lame excuses would count forever."

"I never, **never** wanted any of this to touch her."

"An example of that denial."

The anger finally emerged. "Fuck you."

She would take his anger and deal with it. In a few days it would pass, and he would be more accepting of her decision and the reasons for it. Right now, though, he got up and walked away from her, out of the room, to another part of the house. He would continue to do that, too, for a few days. That, and turn his back to her in bed. All she needed to do was be patient. He would soon need her to fill that part of his life that was empty, the emptiness that their work engendered, that they both ran and hid from endlessly.

When Mai was certain she was alone, the door to the office blocking her from being observed, she wept. For the emptiness she rarely escaped and that only Alexei and the woman-child upstairs could fill. She had gone against everything her profession represented. She had been honest with one of the most important people in her life, and as terrible as was the knowledge that honesty imparted to Natalia, she was left with an understanding far more appalling.

Leading Natalia to the knowledge she sought had changed them all, and nothing would ever be the same again.

Blood Vengeance

◆

January 16, 1999
Raçak, Kosovo

The snow-covered hills provided camouflage for the white trucks that wended their way along the hilly road. Only the letters "UN" in contrasting black on each door identified the big, Mercedes cargo trucks. They kicked up no plume of dust on the frozen ground, though the rumble of their diesel engines told the villagers new interlopers were arriving.

Led by a white, UN Bradley Armored Vehicle, the convoy stopped in the heart of Raçak and found empty streets. The trucks' engines idling behind him, the Bradley gunner scanned with his laser-guided aiming system. On the passenger side of the lead truck, a door opened, and a pair of booted feet emerged, the wearer sliding out to land in snow. Wearing the boots was a woman, clad all in black, an easy target against the pale background. Her leather coat, belted at the waist, hung to mid-shin, and she was hatless in the cold, her breath frosting the air in front of her. Behind dark glasses, her eyes mimicked the Bradley gunner and shifted left and right, taking in the vacant streets.

The village hadn't been "cleansed" because its buildings were intact, none burned, none bombed, the mosque undefiled. A chill coursed up the woman's spine, not from the cold but from the possibilities of what had emptied the village. United Nations Representative Maitland "Mai" Fisher walked to the left side of the Bradley where the gunner sat.

"What do you see?" she asked.

The gunner looked at his heat-sensitive display and said, "They're there."

Eyes still on the move, Fisher walked into the full sunlight, where those peering out from their windows could see she was someone they knew. She stood for several long moments, her eyes studying the distant hills, knowing she would never see the sniper, if there were one, and that she would feel the bullet just before she heard the shot.

To her left, something creaked. She turned toward the sound. The dark opening of a doorway framed an older woman in a traditional head scarf. Her eyes, sunk in folds of wrinkles, squinted in the glare from the snow.

"Ah!" the Grandmother exclaimed, then louder, "Ah! Ah!"

She began to shout alternately in Serbo-Croatian and Albanian as she trotted from the doorway toward the woman standing in the middle of the road. When she reached Fisher, the Grandmother clasped Fisher's hands in supplication and babbled, tears streaming down her face.

Then, other women poured from doors all about the street and converged on the two women. Their voices added to the Grandmother's, going beyond Fisher's ability to translate, though her Serbo-Croatian was good. Their intent was obvious, though. They were pointing to something beyond the village, tugging at Fisher's expensive clothes, pushing her in that direction.

"Come, come," said the Grandmother, and Fisher followed. As she did, she looked back over her shoulder and noticed the absence of men.

Old the woman might have been, but her stride was sure-footed. She pushed invariably forward, her vocalizations alternating between pleading exhortations to hurry and gut-wrenching sobs. The Grandmother's weeping increased the closer they came to a small gully with steep sides. Ten meters away, the Grandmother abruptly stopped, covered her eyes with one hand, and dropped to her knees. Her head bowed, she rocked back and forth, pointing toward the gully.

"There, there," she chanted.

Prescient dread in the midst of a bright, winter morning settled on Fisher's shoulders. As she walked in the direction the Grandmother pointed, she felt as if she were trudging up a steep hill. Before she saw anything, she smelled it, hackles rising on her neck. Fisher slipped her right hand under the left side of her coat and brought out a gun. She gripped it two-handed to clear the way before her and continued to approach the gully.

The odors intensified. Not putrefaction. Too cold for that. Gunpowder. Sweat. Feces. Urine. Blood. A combination she knew and well: They were the smells of fear.

Fisher saw a foot minus a shoe, the shoe nearby. Then another foot, its leg, the whole body, then another body and another. The full view of the gully soon lay open to her.

Bodies. Dozens of them. Sprawled. Men and boys. Dark, dried blood on the snow, on their clothing, their faces. Chests blown open. Unseeing eyes staring skyward, slack mouths, pale skin the color of death.

Fisher's knowing eyes studied the lay of the corpses, how they had fallen. The narrowness of the gully hemmed them in so that they lay like fallen dominoes, one torso resting on the legs of the body next to it. Surprisingly little snow was disturbed, and the bodies all had frozen patches of snow on their knees. The soft weeping of the Grandmother the only sound in the forest, Fisher looked up at the crest of the gully and, in her mind's eye, saw the soldiers standing there, their automatic rifles and machine guns pointed down into the narrow wound in the earth.

Her dread evaporated, replaced by rage. Addicted to the taste of blood from their ethnic cleansing in Bosnia and Croatia, Slobodan Milosevic's finest, certainly no more than a day before, had now slaked their cravings, four years unfulfilled, with Kosovars. She could already hear the excuses coming from Belgrade: These people were rebels or aiding rebels or caught in the crossfire between the army and the rebels. And the excuses would be delivered with straight faces, with pleas for understanding of the problems faced by a legitimate government dealing with a rebel liberation army and a populace who supported it in defiance of law.

Fisher turned away from the scene that would haunt her dreams for weeks and walked to the kneeling, crying Grandmother, whose husband, son, and grandson lay dead in the gully. The young woman helped the older one to her feet, embraced her, and steadied her as they walked back to the village where the Grandmother next led her to the mosque. Four more bodies there. They hadn't been killed there, but dragged there to be wept over by women. An age-old story in this part of the world where blood vengeance was the rule of law: Men kill; women weep.

Except the dark eyes of Maitland Fisher no longer wept for the dead.

On the open floor of the mosque, women tended a dozen wounded. The mosque had been tainted after all. Fisher walked to and knelt by a prepubescent boy, shot in the leg. She examined the makeshift bandage, lifting it to peer at the wound. The boy would live, but the leg was beyond saving. As she replaced the cloth covering the ruined leg, she smiled in encouragement. Eyes red-rimmed and fatigued, a beleaguered woman stroking the boy's brow looked up at the visitor.

"My son," she said, defeat in her voice.

The boy looked up at Fisher, too, then he murmured something to his mother.

"He asked, are you the Angel of Bosnia?" the mother said.

"No, I'm no angel," Fisher said with the shadow of a smile.

"You know who did this?" the mother said, defeat replaced by defiance. The women exchanged a look, the mother's eyes asking Fisher for something.

Fisher nodded and stood. The Grandmother plucked at her sleeve again.

"I tell everyone," the Grandmother said, pointing to the bodies that had been dragged from the gully, "to leave them out there so world can see."

And the world would see, for with the international observers and investigators later that day came the international press, with their cameras recording the horror and the humanity of a previously unknown and unheralded Raçak, the world's latest killing ground.

* * *

2

February 27, 1999

Belgrade, Yugoslavia

The soldier woke with a big head. Certainly not the first warrior in such a condition nor the last. As painful consciousness returned to him, he recalled how he had gotten the hangover. There had been a woman, of course. A dark-haired, dark-eyed woman. Older than he but good-looking, excited by his uniform, by the way he looked in it.

He had been granted his first liberty in months, and he and his friends had needed release from duty, honor, and country. While the diplomats talked in France, the soldiers had hopped among the bars, enjoyed the applause and free drinks offered to heroic defenders of the Serb Republic, and prowled for easy women. Youngest and best-looking, Djavo Ladic had been the first to find one such woman, a European, wealthy by her clothes and jewelry. From the beginning of their encounter, she had made it obvious it was Djavo who piqued her interest, so his comrades had drifted away, envious and anticipating the tales he would tell.

Heady from his first battles, Djavo and the woman had drunk and talked and laughed as, all the while, she had let him take liberties, and then more. So much so, Djavo had worried he'd drunk too much, but, then, he'd been six months without this kind of woman, a willing one. Like his fellow soldiers, he had taken women in many of the villages they had cleansed, but that had been as easy as taking their meager belongings. They were the spoils of war, but now he was sensing, albeit distantly, that what he wanted from this woman could not be had by force, that it would be better not that way. And this woman was older, more experienced, and so could help him if he lagged.

At just after two in the morning, they had reeled into her hotel room, and she had pulled his great coat down off his shoulders, trapping his arms. Her mouth closed on his, her tongue insistent. Djavo had wanted to free his arms so that he could pull her clothes away, but her grip had been unyielding. Now, there was only the hangover and no clear memory of their coupling. He hoped the woman was still around and wanted him as much in the daylight as maybe she had in the dark. To wake himself fully, Djavo stretched.

And found he could not move.

No, he could move, but his movements were limited. As awareness now rushed in, he felt the restraints on his wrists and ankles. He tested them again, and they tightened.

"Fight them, and they get tighter," confirmed the woman's voice.

Djavo swallowed down his panic. He was a soldier after all. Maybe the woman liked this kind of thing. What was it called? Bondage. Djavo remembered her, dressed in black, wearing a long, black leather coat. Yes, that was it. That thought warming his groin, he opened his eyes. He stared at his lap and realized he was bound, naked, to a chair. The headache pounded now, but he lifted his head, willing his eyes to focus.

The woman sat across from him, lounging in a much more comfortable chair than the hard one he was tied to. One of her legs was crossed over the other, swinging at the knee. In her hands were a cup and saucer, and she sipped daintily from the cup. She was dressed the same as the night before, though she looked none the worst for the wear for all she had drunk. His own head now clear of drink, Djavo realized she had consumed very little alcohol though she had been generous in buying him round after round. Panic began to rise again.

"This is what you like, yes?" he asked, a smile on his dry lips, his voice hoarse.

She gave him no reply. Djavo watched her set the teacup aside and fix a stare on him.

"What is this, then?" Djavo asked, some of the bully coming back, the bluster that brought fear to the Kosovars he encountered.

"Requital," she replied.

"For what?"

"Raçak."

"Raçak? I wasn't there."

"Lie to me, and you make it worse."

"Why do you care about Raçak?" The woman said nothing but continued to stare. "I won't talk about Raçak," Djavo insisted.

"Then, as I said, so much the worse for you," the woman replied. She stood, and Djavo looked up at her. The night before her face had been alight with laughter and sexual excitement, her eyes bright and glassy. This morning they were expressionless. She reached into a pocket and took out a small knife, thumbing its blade out.

"I see that you're not circumcised, Djavo," she said, leaning over him and holding the knife in front of his face. Her voice was low, almost a whisper, so only he could hear.

Djavo laughed nervously. She had to be joking, but her eyes told him she wasn't.

"You're crazy," he said.

"And what is lining up people in a gully and back-shooting them?" she replied.

"I told you, I wasn't there."

"You're lying. You told me last night your unit was there."

The blade was between them as a reminder, close enough for Djavo to see the well-honed edge.

"My unit was there," he said, compressing his lips to hold back the terror that welled yet again. "But I did no shooting. I stayed back in the village."

"Give me the names."

Djavo shook his head.

"They were in your unit. You know them. I'm not practiced at this type of surgery, you know. One little slip, and, well, there goes the next generation of Ladics."

"I'm a soldier," Djavo insisted. "I only obey my orders. The men who did…" Djavo hesitated. He was being truthful. He had not participated in the shooting at Raçak, though some of his friends had. As per the standing orders, all males of military age had been gathered and marched away from Raçak, Djavo and others remaining behind to keep the villagers in line. He had heard the automatic weapons fire and seen his comrades return, their demeanor excited. He hadn't had his suspicions confirmed until they boasted and bragged later.

The woman raised an eyebrow at him. "Which men?" she asked, her eyes leaving his to look at his penis, then the knife, then back at him. He pursed his lips again to keep the words from tumbling out and gave a single negative shake of his head.

"Do you know who I am?" the woman asked him. "I have a name in Bosnia, given to me by some of your compatriots who 'followed orders' there."

Djavo's eyes flickered. He hadn't served in the Army during Bosnia, having only joined a year before. Some of the veterans had told him a of a UN relief worker whom the Bosnians called the Angel of Bosnia for her efforts. The militias, however, because of her unrelenting pursuit of them by legal means and otherwise, called her the Angel of Death.

"My God," Djavo prayed.

"That's right. I am your god now, Djavo, with all the powers of life and death. To save your life, you give me names."

"And you'll do what? Kill them?"

The woman seemed surprised at that suggestion. "Of course not. I work for the War Crimes Tribunal. The Danes and Finns are investigating the forensic evidence from Raçak, and when they reach the inevitable conclusion, we'll need names. Do you know why men are circumcised when they're babies, Djavo? Because there are relatively few blood vessels in the penis then. I could be completely successful in removing only the foreskin, but you could bleed to death here, tied up naked in a chair. What an ignoble end for a soldier. What a way to be found by the hotel maid. The soldier, the man of action, though a little less manly than he used to be."

He looked into her eyes again. She had done this before, been close to someone she had killed. He read it there, as he had read it in the eyes of his fellow soldiers.

"In Raçak we were met by Serbian Special Forces," Djavo said. "They had already picked out the rebels from the village, and they asked for the unit's veterans."

His eyes on the knife, he rattled off their names.

"My sergeant passed me over," he continued. "The others, they were Special Forces," Djavo emphasized. "We were never told their names."

"Did anyone address their leader by rank."

"Major."

The woman straightened, holding the knife at her side. "Any Spec Ops major will do, then," she murmured and walked out of Djavo's sight.

"What…what are you going to do with me?" he stammered.

"Let you go," she replied from behind him.

"You're lying."

"Lying? No, not now. I lied when I said I wanted you, but you didn't seem to notice. By the way, if you're thinking about reporting this…"

She switched on the room's television/VCR, and Djavo saw a familiar figure, himself, trussed to the chair and spilling his guts. She would see to it his unit got a copy, maybe even the Special Forces. She stopped the tape and removed it from the VCR, then walked out of his sight again. Djavo shivered as he felt her hand on the back of his neck, her breath there as she leaned down again. One of his hands was suddenly free; she had cut his bonds, but the knife point was back at his throat.

"Just take it easy," she said. "I'll be leaving now. You can finish untying yourself. Your clothes are here. Get dressed and forget this, but you have my permission to tell your friends I was the best you ever had."

The point of the knife left his throat. When he got up the courage to turn his head, she was gone.

*   *   *

3
March 22, 1999
Kosovar Refugee Camp, Albania

The tradition was for another male family member to take in her and her son now that her husband was dead, but with only one leg, her son moved so slowly on his crutches. The mother feared they would never reach her husband's uncle. She was a strong woman, but the boy was 12 and growing. No longer could she carry him, and when she tried, it only humiliated him.

UN doctors had amputated his injured leg above the knee, and the woman—the relief worker—who had brought the news of Raçak to the world had made sure the boy had medicines and the crutches. On the woman's last visit to Raçak, she had promised a prosthesis, but then the boy and his mother had fled along with many others, seeking security with relatives in Albania. It was now spring, though a fresh snowfall added to the refugees' woes. No help came from Albania, whose government had to keep them at arm's length and insist they were illegals or risk the might of the Yugoslavian Army, now running unchecked over

Kosovo, being turned on them. There was only the food people could carry with them, and most of that had been confiscated at the border.

At first when the mother heard trucks approaching, she thought they were Yugoslavian tanks, defying the border and coming to kill them all. It was her son who reassured her by his excited hopping on one leg, a crutch held in the air.

"It's her, it's her," he shouted to his mother.

Wearily, the mother stood up from her makeshift tent and shielded her eyes against the snow-glare. UN trucks. At least there would be food and blankets.

"It's just relief workers," the mother told her son.

"She said she would come," the boy insisted. "Can I go see?"

"No."

"How will she know where we are?"

"It was a promise made from guilt, like all the westerners," the mother said. "They promise but do nothing. Don't get your hopes up."

Even as she said it, the mother studied the people emerging from the trucks. The refugees surged toward them, and the mother put a hand on her son's shoulder to keep him back.

Then, she was there. The woman. Dressed in black again, the same long, leather coat. She stood in the midst of the ragged humanity who reached out to her. The mother watched as the woman made her away across the camp.

"I'm no angel," she had once said, but she was the very image of it now, the mother thought.

Beside the woman limped a man who carried beneath his arm a box perhaps a meter long. He and the woman peered searchingly at the faces of the people as they strode through the camp. The mother felt her son slip from her grasp, watched him move forward on his crutches to meet the woman. She must have heard his shout because she suddenly looked toward him and smiled broadly. The mother watched as her son reached the woman's side, and the woman stroked his hair, leaving her hand on his shoulder until they arrived at the quilt the mother had suspended between two trees for their shelter.

"Mother," the woman greeted. "I came back to Raçak and was told you had left. I didn't think I would find you."

"It was too dangerous there," the mother replied.

The woman indicated her companion. "This is a friend of mine from America," she said. "We have something for the boy."

The man smiled and opened the box he had been carrying. Inside was a prosthetic leg, small; a child's leg. The mother thought that it was both the ugliest thing she had ever seen and the most beautiful.

"I lost my leg in Africa," the man explained. "I stepped on a land mine. I can show the boy how to put this on, take it off, care for it."

"I have no money," the mother said.

"It's a gift," the woman assured. "And if you tell me where you're going to live, I'll make sure he gets others as he grows." The woman leaned down to the boy, who was wide-eyed and struggling not to weep. "If you go with my friend," the woman told him, "he'll teach you all about this."

The boy nodded and looked to his mother. She hesitated. Trust was the first thing she had lost after the Serbs came to her village on a cold, January morning, but today hope constricted her throat. She nodded. The man closed the box and motioned the boy to follow him. Alone, the two women regarded each other much as they had in the mosque two months before.

"I have something for you, too," the woman told the mother.

"For me, I want nothing."

"You'll want this."

The woman reached inside her leather coat, withdrew a package wrapped in brown paper, and held it out toward the mother. The mother took it and cautiously began to unwrap the paper.

On the day when hell came to Raçak, the Yugoslavian Special Forces had arrived first, clad in their winter camouflage—white pants and white pullover shirts with hoods, just like the one the mother held up. Except this one was drenched in fresh blood that soaked the front of the garment as if the wearer's throat...

The women looked at each other again, and the mother knew this was what she had asked for without words, what no woman could ask for in her culture, the traditional blood vengeance. The mother had asked this stranger, this woman, for it because the mother no longer had a husband to avenge her son.

"And what will you do?" the mother asked, unknowingly echoing a hapless Serb soldier. "Kill them all?"

"No," the woman said. "One was enough."

The mother asked, "Why for my son?"

"It wasn't only for your son."

The mother struggled with the implications of her break with tradition. "Why?" she repeated.

"I'll never know why," the woman replied, her eyes moist. "I came to the Balkans a decade ago to try to bring peace. I hate it here, and I love it. It made me what I am."

The mother looked down at her trophy once more then folded it carefully and re-wrapped it in the paper. She knelt down and tucked it away in the suitcase she had carried from Raçak. She turned around to thank the woman, but the mother saw her walking away, again engulfed by other refugees, their outstretched hands trying to touch her but sliding off the black leather coat without gaining purchase.

A Father's No Shield for His Child

◆

November 6
Washington, DC

To keep warm in the chill November day, William Henry Munro paced. There was a drizzle falling, and though his overcoat was warm and waterproof, his head was bare. The tips of his ears were uncomfortably cold and, he suspected, as red as his chapped cheeks. At 42 he was of an age where a man started to get vain about his looks, worried about his hair, concerned about his weight, but Munro had a thick head of hair, salt and pepper in color, cut conservatively, and was lean and fit. A few women he'd dated had called him attractive, never handsome, and he couldn't judge for himself. His northern European skin, sensitive to cold and heat, had always vexed him. A quarter hour in either temperature extreme, and his complexion took on the cast of a 24-hour drunk. On a day like today, in addition to the ruddiness, his eyes would water and his nose would run.

On cue, he reached for his handkerchief, to keep his upper lip from embarrassment, and glanced around again, his eyes seeking.

The dismal day hadn't deterred tourists from the Vietnam Veterans Memorial. It was the weekend before Veterans Day, and there were several commemorative events planned. People were arriving early, having impromptu reunions, and placing their remembrances at the wall of black granite etched with names from another generation. Munro had missed out on Vietnam, his birth date making him eligible for the lottery, not the draft, and he'd drawn a high lottery number. Plus, he'd been in college in 1975 when the U.S. retreated from Saigon. He was among that group of baby boomers who had never entered military service because they didn't have to. He had weathered the derision of the vets in his workplace who deemed him incapable of his job because he had not soldiered, but he had been a Secret Service Agent for more than 20 years, with the requisite promotions occurring exactly when they should have. The old guys were retired, and the Secret Service itself was more reflective of America than it used to be. To Munro that was a good thing, even if a few holdovers from the old days thought otherwise.

A breeze stirred and chilled him even more. The woman had said she would meet him between 1300 and 1330 at the Vietnam Women's Memorial on the high ground above the black slash in the earth that was The Wall. He checked his watch. 1326. Munro began to scan again, intending to turn through a full 360 degrees, if necessary. He was certain he could recognize her, even though she had told him to purchase one of the crepe paper poppies from a vendor on the grounds of the memorial and put it on his right lapel. Just like a couple hundred other folks wandering around.

Then, a movement among dozens of others caught his eye, and he looked toward the Washington Monument. A woman was striding toward the Vietnam Memorial, a purposeful swing to her arms, an appealing swing to her hips. She was dressed all in black and wearing a supple leather trench coat that was unbelted. It was a gray, overcast day, but she wore sunglasses that wrapped around her face. Her hair was loose, and as she got closer Munro saw she was little changed in three and a half years. Her dark hair was streaked gray but just at the temples, a striking feature, so striking he wondered if she affected it. He remembered her to be unassuming about her appearance and decided the streaks were natural. The set of her mouth was firm, and though he couldn't see her eyes, Munro had the impression she didn't want to be here. She was distinct and attractive enough that she turned a few heads, including Munro's, but he also remembered she was married. She strode up to within five feet of him and stood still, hands at her sides, waiting.

"Ms. Fisher?" Munro said, extending his right hand. "Good to see you again."

Her face was unchanged, but her silence went on long enough that Munro thought she didn't recognize him.

"I was the one who…" Munro began.

"Yes," she said. "At the hospital. You picked me up there to take me to the President."

Four days after the Oklahoma City Bombing, the President had spoken at a memorial service there and had requested this woman's presence. Munro had had to take her from her husband's hospital bed. She and her husband had both been injured trying to stop the domestic terrorism, her husband worse than she, and she had been reluctant to leave him, unwilling to surrender the weapon Munro knew she carried. "Am I under arrest?" she had asked when Munro insisted.

"I didn't remember your name, Agent Munro," she continued, and Munro recalled he had liked her voice, with its high-class British accent but American vernacular.

"Hank," he said, his hand still extended. She shook it firmly, and her hand was toasty warm through her glove and his.

"Ms. Fisher, can we go somewhere and talk?"

"We are somewhere, Agent Munro, and until I know why the Secret Service wants to talk to me, I prefer the open. If this is about the Lewinsky thing, not only do I know absolutely nothing, I can't be compelled to testify about it."

Munro flushed in embarrassment. "No, it's nothing to do with that. The Secret Service doesn't want to talk to you. I do."

He saw her forehead crease in a frown. "This request didn't come from the President?"

"No."

"It came to my Director with a national security protocol."

Munro shifted his feet uncomfortably. "I'm, ah, afraid I've used some agency resources for a personal matter," he said.

"The President's personal matters are not an assignment for the UN, and I don't work on private concerns."

"It's not the President's personal matters."

"Agent Munro, you had better start explaining yourself quickly because my Director is going to be interested in why he had to summon me from a mission in Bosnia because the request for my services had the highest priority attached to it."

"I wouldn't have gone through official channels, but when I asked around to some people in your, ah, business, on how to contact you, they were pretty mum."

"That's why we're spies. You've got two more minutes of my time, Agent Munro."

Munro glanced around. Several people had noticed the electricity between them and were watching. They had both kept their voices low, but body language spoke volumes.

"I feel exposed here," he pleaded. "I would rather speak somewhere privately."

"Ninety seconds."

"Ms. Fisher, please, I used the protocol because it was the only way I could be assured I could speak to **you**."

"About what?"

"A personal matter. One that I'd rather discuss in private."

"When you start talking in circles you forfeit your time. Good day, Agent Munro."

She turned and took two steps away. Munro elevated his voice slightly, just enough that only she would hear, and spoke a name. She stopped abruptly and turned back to him. They stared at each other, neither giving way. Munro felt the chill enter his bones, and he knew he was about to shiver. Unable to stop it, a shudder coursed through him, and he saw Fisher remove her sunglasses. Her eyes were dark, lightly made up, and full of suspicion.

"There's a Starbucks at Farragut Square," she said. "I have to move my car. Meet me there in 15 minutes." Munro didn't move, and she canted her eyebrows inquiringly.

"How do I know you'll show up?" he asked.

"Because I've just said so. I'll have a grande skim latte and a blue-berry scone. Fifteen minutes," she said and walked off the way she came.

Munro was at 18th and F before he realized she had given him a food order.

∗   ∗   ∗

When Munro turned around with the tray containing two lattes and two scones, he saw Mai Fisher had entered unnoticed by him and was seated at the high counter that faced onto the park at Farragut Square. He hesitated momentarily then walked over to her. She had removed her sunglasses and gloves, and they lay on the counter. Munro set the tray next to them and seated himself on the chair next to her.

"They're identical orders," he said, tugging his gloves off, wanting nothing more than to wrap his cold fingers around the hot cup of liquid. He did so, inhaling the steam and feeling it warm his nose.

"See the gentleman in the gray coat in the park?" Mai Fisher asked him.

Munro looked where she indicated. A severely crew cut man in his late 30's sat on a bench so that he looked directly into Starbucks. He had on a military style overcoat and was hatless. His posture was relaxed, one leg casually thrown over the other, an arm resting on the back of the park bench. When he saw Munro looking at him, he nodded once.

"That's my husband's nephew," Fisher said. "Late of the Spetsnas, currently assigned as my bodyguard. If he receives the signal from me he and I agreed upon, you're a dead man."

Munro choked on his coffee.

"Christ," he said, using some napkins to sop up what he'd spilled on his coat. He looked angrily at Fisher, who sipped her latte casually, as if she'd made mention of the ill weather. "What do you think I want with you?"

"Well, I don't know, do I? You wanted privacy. We have it."

"Why do you have a bodyguard?"

"General Ratko Mladic of the Serb Army would like to see that I don't put a crimp into any more of his ethnic cleansing plans. There was a recent attempt in Zagreb. My husband is in The Hague, and he worries." She shrugged, again casually, as if every married couple worried about murder attempts on each other.

Munro glanced at the gray-coated man then back to Fisher. "What did you call him? Spats…"

"Spetsnas," she corrected. "Formerly the Soviet Special Forces. There were two kinds. Shock troop and assassin. After the 1991 coup attempt, they became Yeltsin's personal security. Now, they've officially been disbanded."

"Which one was he?" Fisher raised an eyebrow. "Oh." He drank some more latte. "Well, I'm not on a Serbian General's payroll," Munro said, forcing a smile. Fisher didn't respond to the humor.

"Agent Munro, you mentioned Eamon Cill Chainnigh. That's a name I haven't heard in a long time, so I'm quite curious why you're mentioning an IRA hit man to me." She gave the Irish name its Gaelic pronunciation.

"I'm Irish," Munro began.

She laughed slightly. "So claims 90% of America with a vaguely Irish last name."

"No, I **am** Irish. **Was** Irish. I was born there. My parents came to America when I was two and became citizens."

"Are you Eamon's long lost cousin that he's hit up for money or guns?"

"No."

Fisher stared at him, waiting, not seeing the inner turmoil, which he'd been masking from everyone for days.

"Well, Agent Munro, I'm Irish, too. Still am. Now that we have that in common, tell me how you know Eamon Cill Chainnigh."

"Kilkenny has kidnapped a U.S. citizen in Ireland, and he contacted me."

"Kidnapping of a U.S. citizen is not a matter for the UN. I believe you want your brothers at the FBI."

"I'm aware of that."

"Have you contacted them?"

"No."

"Why?"

"Kilkenny said he would kill the person if I did."

Fisher's expression was incredulous. "You've been an SSA for what, 15, 20 years?"

"Twenty-two."

"And you bought that line?"

"You don't understand."

"That's what we're here for, isn't it? For you to explain it to me."

"It was Kilkenny's suggestion that I contact you."

"My last dealings with Cill Chainnigh were more than 13 years ago, and I haven't worked Ireland since. Not even the Omagh bombing. Besides, Cill Chainnigh didn't know me as Mai Fisher. The person he thought I was is 'dead.'"

"He said, 'Tell her I finally know she survived Lifford.'"

Fisher set her coffee down and leaned back in her chair, staring across the coffee shop.

"Fuck," she muttered. She turned her eyes back on Munro. He had a distinct memory of her eyes from Oklahoma City. They were expressive, emotive. The gaze she gave him now was flat, bereft of humanness. "I know the kidnapped citizen is neither my husband nor my step-granddaughter," she said. "I spoke with my husband this morning, about two hours before I met you, and my step-granddaughter is at my house with her au pair. If it were the President's daughter, it would be all over the news, and it can't be somebody important to me because I've already mentioned the only two people who matter."

"No, the person doesn't matter to you. She matters to me," Munro said quietly.

Fisher shook her head and gave a low chuckle. "What was it?" she asked. "An exchange program with the Garda? You met a little piece over in Ireland that you just had to have, and now they're claiming that she's 'kidnapped' to exact something from you. Open your eyes, Munro. You've been had. They knew you were Secret Service, so they knew you'd have the means to contact me. I'm not playing their little game, and neither should you. Thanks for the coffee, and say hello to the President for me. I'll forego mentioning this to my Director."

She stood up, and without hesitation, Munro put his hand on her arm, not heavily but not lightly either.

"Please, Ms. Fisher, let me finish the story. The woman is not a 'piece' I had. I was trying to explain. This has been very difficult for me. Something out of my control, that I couldn't go to my superiors for. Maybe I should have. That's the way I'm trained, but something else took over. I couldn't react as a Secret Service Agent because I had to react as a…" Emotion stopped him. He watched her peer deeply into his face.

"As a what?" she prompted.

Munro swallowed and found his voice. "As a father."

Munro found he had to compose himself and that he hadn't taken his hand off Fisher's arm. She lay her hand over his and gripped his fingers. He stared at the hand, wide palm, short fingers that were ring-less with a French manicure. Again, he felt the heat emanating.

"Forget the coffee," she said, quietly. "The Hay-Adams is down the street. You need a drink."

∗   ∗   ∗

A $50 bill told the host she wanted privacy, and he obliged by seating Mai Fisher and her guest in a secluded corner of the Hay-Adams' lounge. The tall man in the gray, military coat, who had followed them, sat at the bar and ordered black coffee though Mai smiled a bit when he glanced at her and tapped his throat with his index finger, a Russian's indication that what he really wanted was vodka. After they were seated, Mai took her coat off and watched as Munro did the same but only after Mai's actions reminded him. They sat quietly after Mai gave the drink order and didn't speak until after the two Irish coffees had been brought and sipped from.

"Imagine my surprise," Munro said, "when I tried to order one of these in Ireland, and they stared at me as if I was nuts."

Mai smiled at him. "The Irish don't like to dilute their whiskey. Irish coffee started in San Francisco, about as far from Ireland as you can get. I, however, have a weakness for them."

"Me, too." He drank some more, and she waited. She had pushed him hard earlier and now regretted it. She would let him set the pace.

"I was married when I was in college," Munro began, "back in the days when you still made an honest woman out of your girlfriend when your birth control method failed."

"Happens in the best of families," Mai said. Munro gave her a curious look. "Why do you think I'm married?" she added.

Munro tried to grin. "What, did you have to make an honest man out of your husband?"

Her smile broadened. "Something like that."

"Well, the pregnancy lasted longer than the marriage, and my ex had custody for a couple of years then decided it cramped her style as a Grateful Dead groupie. So, I raised our daughter."

"Just you?"

"Yep."

"A single father in the Secret Service. It's a wonder they didn't drum you out or something."

"It was difficult, and there were times I should have put her first, but we worked it out. We're father and daughter, but we're buddies, too. You know how it is."

Actually, she didn't. Her child had died at birth, but she decided Munro didn't need to know that.

"I had a lot of help from my mother when Deidre was little, and when I decided to finish out my career here in DC, she opted to study at Catholic University. She had her own place, but we were still close, you know. I saw her, see her every day."

Mai watched as Munro gripped the coffee mug two-handed and wondered if he were still cold from the weather or from his encounter with IRA madness.

"This past Spring," he continued, "her Contemporary Literature class assigned the book, *Angela's Ashes*. You know the one?"

Mai nodded. She knew its author, but again she suspected Munro wasn't interested.

"She knew she was half Irish," Munro continued. "It was just never a big deal until she read that book, then she just had to go. She and I went on Spring break. She went for two weeks over the summer, then applied for and was accepted in an exchange program with Trinity College for this semester." Munro's smile was unforced as he remembered. "We were running up the trans-Atlantic phone bills, let me tell you." He sobered again, took a long drink of his Irish coffee, finishing it, and sat quietly, the smile gone, and a haunting on his face.

Get on with it, Mai wanted to say, but she realized he was still setting the pace. The host caught her eye from across the room and raised an eyebrow inquiringly. Mai pointed to the Irish coffees and held up two fingers.

"Five days ago," Munro said with a sigh. "I get this call from her. I have to come over and right away, but she won't say why. She was trying to be nonchalant, but this is my kid, you know. I can read her nuances even 3,000 miles away. Then, this man comes on the phone, gives me a time and a place in Dublin, and tells me not to contact the FBI, the Garda, or anyone else." Munro looked at her, his face pained. "Then I heard her scream," he said, his throat constricting.

Mai put her hand on Munro's wrist as the waiter approached. She looked over at the bar where her nephew was asking his own question with his eyes. Almost imperceptibly, she shook her head to tell him everything was all right. More or less. Alone again, Mai released Munro's arm and urged his drink toward him. He was Irish, after all. Whiskey would only lubricate his mouth.

"Don't misunderstand my question, Agent Munro," Mai said. "How do you know she's still alive?"

"They have called me twice since I was there, and I get to talk to her. And I know it's her, not a recording."

"Are you sure?"

"Yes," he said, a bit defensively.

"When's the next call due?"

"Tonight."

"So, what happened at the meet?"

"Kilkenny let me see her in a car. She had C4 strapped to her, and Kilkenny had the detonator on a dead man's switch."

"Semtex," Mai said.

"What?"

"Not C4. The U.S. has too tight a control on that. The IRA use Semtex. And to be somewhat fair, Cill Chainnigh is not IRA anymore. He's a breakaway, still fighting his own little war."

"I thought you didn't work Ireland anymore."

"I don't, but I still get briefings and do an occasional consult. Describe to me the man who said he was Cill Chainnigh."

Munro gave her a puzzled look but complied. "About 5'7", 5'8". Mid-60's. Bald on top. White hair with some red still in it. Grey eyes. Fleshy. On his cheeks, what do they call them, the red veins?"

"Spider veins. Likely to occur on most heavy drinking Irishmen starting in their 50's."

"Yes. Red nose."

That would be Eamon, Mai thought. When she'd encountered him, he'd been in his early 50's already beginning to go to seed, so Munro's description fit. No photo, not even a surveillance one, had been seen of him since 1985, and the British Home Service and the SAS considered him dead.

"At the meet, is that where he first mentioned me?" she asked.

"Yes. I mean, I thought he wanted money or for me to facilitate a shipment of guns or something along those lines," Munro said. "What he told me was that message I mentioned and that I do whatever I could to get you to Ireland by November 11th, or my daughter would die." He looked at Mai. "What is November 11th? He insisted upon that."

Mai didn't want to confide that deeply in Munro, but he was a father with a child's life in the balance. He wouldn't conform to her dismissals.

She explained, "November the 11th will be the 13th anniversary of an explosion that destroyed a farm house in Lifford, County Donegal, just over the border from Northern Ireland. Nine IRA people died. One person survived."

"And you had something to do with it?" Munro asked.

Letting her memory walk into an area she wanted to avoid, she replied, "In a manner of speaking."

"I would like non-dissembling answers," Munro said.

"Leave it at that, Munro."

"I can't. A man kidnaps my daughter and asks me for you. I need to know why."

They locked eyes, Munro's gray-green eyes staring into hers. She could see that any counterfeiter or threatener of the President would be intimidated by that glare, but she had been stared at by monsters who only wore human skin. It failed to alarm her.

"Munro, again, don't misunderstand me. I have to ask this question. Are you absolutely certain she has truly been kidnapped?"

Munro's stare grew hostile. "What the fuck does that mean?"

"It's happened before, Agent Munro. A starry-eyed American, usually a girl, goes to the Old Sod to find her roots. She runs into a strikingly good looking young man who impresses her with his charm and gift of the gab. Pretty soon the talk moves to the Cause, and she gets suckered in. She's probably talked about you, so the fact that you're a Secret Service Agent with access to certain people is something her new friends can use. They pass that info along to Cill Chainnigh, and your daughter gets convinced to go along with a kidnapping charade."

"It was not a charade. I know my daughter."

"You were distraught, not seeing things clearly…"

"I know my daughter," he interrupted, his teeth clenched. "I know every expression of her face and what they mean. She was fucking scared to death. She was not acting. You said you're a mother. You understand what I'm saying."

Mai stared across the lounge. Had he lived, her son would be 21 years old, and she still occasionally indulged the fantasy of what he would look like.

"All right, Agent Munro," she said, looking back at him. "It's a real kidnapping. I just had to ask. I had to make you think about it, so you could be sure."

His angry stare subsided as he comprehended the point of her questions.

"I'm sorry," he said.

"No problem. What did Cill Chainnigh specifically tell you to do?"

"If I bring you to Sligo by the 11th, to a place he'll advise me of, he'll tell you and only you where my daughter is."

"In exchange for what?"

"You," Munro said, very quietly. "Unless we can work out some way to find her first."

Mai's eyes widened. "You think I can pull that information out of my back pocket?"

"You have resources…"

"Yes, that I can access officially. This not official despite the fact that you used national security protocol. I told you, I haven't worked in Ireland for a long time. Any sources I had are long gone, or they think I'm dead. Have you put a trace on any of the calls?"

"You know what that takes."

"Christ, man, you know how to manipulate the system."

"Of course, but Kilkenny has been very careful to keep the communication well under the time it takes to trace a trans-Atlantic call."

"Cill Chainnigh is a smart man."

Munro gave her another puzzled look.

"He's a bastard," she said, "but a smart one. After Lifford he left Ireland for years, lived in Libya, East Germany, North Korea, China. I'm surprised he'd risk setting foot on the island again. But why the 13th anniversary?" Mai mused. She ran some scenarios through her head. "Unless he won't be around for the 14th," she added.

"I really need for you to tell me some more about this event," Munro said.

"I can't."

"You won't. I can tell the difference. I need to know. This is my goddamned daughter." Her stare back at him was unrelenting. "He doesn't say how I deliver you. He even said if I brought your body to him, that he'd tell me where Deidre is."

"And how would you propose to get my body across an ocean and into another country?" she said.

"I don't know, but I'd fucking find a way by the 11th."

"Think about it, Agent Munro. At the right look from me, Kolya over there manages to make it look like you've had a heart attack."

"And my daughter dies, and it's your fault."

Ah, fuck, he had to say that, but she replied, "So what?"

"You won't let that happen. You try to save lives. You tried to stop that bombing three years ago. You won't let an innocent girl die for something you did 13 years ago."

"You have no idea what I did 13 years ago."

"Then you better tell me so I'll understand why my daughter has to die because you're scared of Eamon Kilkenny."

"Is that what you think it is?"

"What else could it be?"

"That won't work, Agent Munro."

"Then, what's the harm?"

"You think Cill Chainnigh is going to clap me on the back and say, 'No hard feelings, old girl?'"

"Tell me what you did that made Kilkenny take my daughter to get to you," Munro insisted.

Something about Munro's posture had alerted Kolya, and he was slowly approaching. Instead of waving him off, Mai let him come up to the table. He hooked a chair from another table with his foot, spun it around, and sat on it backwards. He stared at Munro, but he spoke in Russian to Mai.

"I don't like the way this looks, totya," he said.

Mai responded in the same language. "I have it under control, Kolya, but just stare at him a bit in that way you have," she said.

"You think that scares me," Munro said to Mai. "Threatening glares, talking in Russian. From what some folks in the FBI told me, you don't need decorative muscle to get your way."

"Decorative?" Kolya said in English. "My muscles are real. My uncle," Kolya said, pointing to himself, "does not like it when people threaten his wife." He pointed to Mai. "Since I obey my uncle in all things, I think you better be more—what is word, totya?" He said something in Russian.

"Civil," Mai translated.

"Yes. Ciwil. I think you better be more ciwil. I will go back to bar now," he said, and did just that.

"Look," Munro said, "if you want him to kill me, just do it, because if somebody kills my kid, I don't want to live. I don't have anything to lose."

Mai watched his intense face, his eyes a little rheumy from the two Irish coffees.

"A man with nothing to lose is dangerous," she said.

"Fucking A." He blinked and sat back in his chair. "They made these Irish coffees a bit strong."

"Fucking A," Mai replied. "Have you ever done any undercover work?"

"No."

"I went undercover in the IRA for nearly six months," she said. "My organization, my husband, the British government, everyone except me thought it was a suicide mission. I had to get in and secure enough trust that I could learn who was receiving a 40-pound shipment of Semtex. Do you have any idea how much destruction 40 pounds of Semtex can cause? Not one big blast. Lots of small ones. In train stations. Shopping malls. Ascot. Wimbledon. The British government knew it had been purchased, and they also knew where it would be delivered, but intercepting it was not enough. They wanted to know which cell was going to get it and who in the Export Office facilitated the deal."

"That was your job?"

"Yes. I spent months establishing my character before I ever arrived in Ireland. The person I was supposed to be, her father and Cill Chainnigh were lads together, and he welcomed me. I found I was able to get him hooked. Most Irishmen are a bloody sentimental lot, terrorist or no, and Eamon trusted me like he would a daughter. He was officer commanding of our 10-person cell. He never stayed with us at the farmhouse. For security, he was always on the move, but he did show up one day, with the Semtex, and stored it in the basement of the house."

Munro's eyes widened. "Jesus," he said, "no wonder it blew up."

"Semtex is a bit more unstable than C4, and under the right conditions, it'll sweat nitroglycerine, but it needed some help. Part of the shipment was detonators."

Mai stopped and drank down some of her coffee. It was near the bottom of the mug, where the sugar and whiskey were strongest. She had so long ago put this out of her mind, and it had been replaced with other horrors, fresher ones, each superseded by another.

"Cill Chainnigh trusted me so much, he put me in charge of the shipment," she said, again staring off across the room as she remembered. "It wasn't one of my regular report-in opportunities, so I couldn't leave the place and meet my contact without causing suspicion. I was hung out by myself, left by the British Home Services to my own devices, so I decided what had to be done. Risk 10 lives to make sure hundreds don't die. Even that 10 was too many for me. So, I decided only one person need die." She looked back at Munro and swallowed the last drop of her drink. "Because the Semtex was in my charge, it was easy to set the detonators and a timer, but I'm not a demolitions expert. I was off a few minutes. I had planned for it to go off while I was the only one in the house. Instead, just the opposite happened. I was outside. Everyone else was inside. I survived. The others died while they were having their morning tea. Because of that 'little' failure, the IRA military council thought it best that Cill Chainnigh leave the country for a while, and he's never quite recovered his position."

She toyed with the empty cup, feeling a familiar yen for cocaine that she quickly quelled.

"So, Agent Munro, that's why he took your daughter. He wants you to bring me to him, so he can have me atone for the nine people I murdered."

"It was an accident," Munro said.

"You sound like someone else," Mai said, with an ironic smile.

"Who?"

"The Oklahoma City bomber said much the same thing to me when I told him the same story. Christ, I never should have gotten started on these," she said, holding up her empty mug. "Do you want another?"

"No."

"Well, then, I'll look like a drunk if I do." She reached into her pocket and dropped a $20 and a $10 bill on the table. From another pocket she took a business card, which she handed to Munro. "Make my day and tell me you taped your conversations."

Munro actually smiled. "I have my head on halfway," he said.

"Good. That's my home address. After your call tonight, come there and bring your tapes. I'll have a few hours to see what I can access quasi-officially."

"Then what?"

"We take my plane to Ireland and fulfill your obligation to Cill Chainnigh with a few modifications of the plan."

"Thank you," he said, and Mai was afraid he was about to weep. If he did that, she'd be blubbering with him, and Kolya would laugh.

"Best not to thank me, yet, because you're going to end up owing me big time."

*   *   *

November 11
Republic of Ireland
   Poets and novelists have often written of the "terrible beauty" of
Ireland, the proud but reactionary people, the attitudes and social con-
ventions slightly behind the rest of the world, the arcane religious
rivalry that defied peace. Mai never thought of the ethnicity that was
three-quarters her heritage as backwards or behind, just peripheral, on
the edges of everything, trying to push to the front but always being
held back by self-imposed limitations.
   Aside from some distant cousins, she was the last in the line of a family whose tree branched back into the pre-Roman days. The surname
had changed over the years but had for two centuries been Maitland,
until her mother had married her father. Maitland was her first name,
and when most people heard it, they understood why she had shortened
it to Mai. Her voice, her upbringing, her education had been English, but
even after years away, she could step from an airplane onto the asphalt of
an Irish airport and hear the bones of her ancestors call to her. To the
Irish, the land is all important, and no matter where you are in the
world, Éirinn will always be home. There was a time when home was
anywhere she and her husband were, but that was too difficult lately.
Unlike her husband, Ireland embraced her unconditionally and did not
care why she had returned or what she was about to do.
   The Northern counties she knew like her own house. The west of the
Republic of Ireland was not so familiar to her, but she knew Sligo had
long been a hotbed of IRA activity, even before the IRA had killed Lord
Louis Mountbatten on his boat in the harbor in 1979. The British government kept a safe house there, used by the British Home Service for
the rare IRA informer, and it took the calling in of only a few favors to
grant Mai the use of it.
   For the few days they had been together, Mai had watched Munro
carefully and saw a man nearly at the limit of his sanity, easily
recognizable because she had been at the edge of hers so often. Alexei,

her absent husband, would chide her for depending on someone so emotionally tied to the situation, but Mai had always believed that strong emotion could be turned to productive use. Though she could tell Munro disliked not being in charge of the situation, she observed as well that he agreed to her single condition: That when they had Cill Chainnigh in their custody, Mai would be wide open to use whatever means necessary to extract information from the IRA man. She could tell that Munro had a moral problem with that, and he hadn't laughed when she suggested Confession afterwards. He did, however, agree. The safety of your children could make you put aside the strongest of qualms.

Someone not familiar with the Irish penchant for vengeance would ask why Cill Chainnigh would go to all this trouble. In addition to holding a grudge for years, Cill Chainnagh had likely found out Mai had a reputation for protecting innocents from harm. Cill Chainnigh knew that Mai would do what was needed to assure that Deidre Munro was safely released. Not that Mai believed for one minute that would happen. The IRA could oftentimes be trusted to release an innocent they used for a purpose, but Cill Chainnigh, beyond conscience, was no longer IRA. His years as a fugitive even from his own people had cemented him as a psychopath, and Deidre Munro was a means to an end, not a person in his eyes. To further his personal agenda, he wouldn't think twice about ordering her death, if he hadn't already. Reality told Mai Deidre Munro was dead from the time Munro told Cill Chainnigh they were on their way to Sligo.

Cill Chainnigh's whole point, Mai knew but did not tell Munro, was to push her to where she would kill him before he gave up Deidre Munro's location, putting another innocent life on her conscience. The nine lives snuffed out at Lifford were not so innocent, and she had dealt with her part in the deaths years ago. Among them were a couple of down-right murderers and others guilty by association. But none of them had harmed her, and Mai had no excuse for killing them. Herself she had been willing to sacrifice and let the authorities deal with the survivors. Everyone from Alexei to the local Garda chief constable had declared it an accident, but she could never be sure. She had survived the explosion but barely, and it had taken her the good part of a year to recover her memory. In reality, she didn't remember setting the charges, but she was the only one who could have. So, she had made no excuses and accepted the responsibility.

She doubted if Cill Chainnigh would excuse her either.

When the time for the meet came and when Cill Chainnigh was so easily taken, it confirmed that was his intention all along. The single bodyguard sitting in a car, subdued without a fight with some knock-out gas. Cill Chainnigh not even resisting the hypodermic she plunged in his neck from behind. Mai had always been suspicious of the easy things, but Munro's hope was so pronounced, he wasn't thinking straight. Once they dumped Cill Chainnigh, cuffed, gagged, and trussed, on the kitchen floor of the safe house, Mai saw Munro visibly relax. He didn't get it.

With Cill Chainnigh unwieldy dead weight, it took the two of them to undress him to his underwear then secure him in a hard kitchen chair. The kitchen was a good choice. Its linoleum floor could easily be cleaned of blood and bodily fluids, and it offered a collection of knives and other sharp implements. Such things had been her husband Alexei's mettle, knives especially. Mai preferred the hands on approach.

*   *   *

For countless minutes, Munro alternated pacing the floor of the kitchen and looking over at Mai Fisher, seated on the bench of a bay window and reading a book. Kilkenny snored lightly on his chair in the middle of the room, and although Munro felt a certain optimism rising in him, he was becoming impatient. Fisher's attitude didn't help. His daughter's life hung in the balance, and Fisher was reading, as if the two of them were on a weekend getaway in the country. Munro had tried to telegraph his contempt for that, but she had ignored him.

This was a strange woman in many ways. So disdainful of him, so quick to dismiss him until he forced her to hear his whole story. Then, she had applied resources she had complained she couldn't use to help him and constantly assured him they would be successful. Even her confidence in her ability to effect a positive outcome irritated Munro. And it didn't seem to matter to her that she rubbed him the wrong way. Maybe that was a measure of her self-assurance, or it was an indication that little mattered to her anymore. Some of both, he decided. She turned a page in her book, and it scraped his nerves raw.

"Goddammit," he swore.

She didn't look up from her book. "Sorry, my reading is so loud," she said, her sarcasm cutting. She glanced up over the book. "Now, you're supposed to say something like, 'How can you possibly read at a time like this?'" Munro said nothing. She dog-eared the page where she left off and looked at Munro, a half-smile on her face.

"Patience, Agent Munro," she said. "Eamon there will be waking in under a quarter of an hour." She tossed the paperback book to him. "If Frank McCourt got your daughter onto her Irish roots, you better not let her read any of that. Seamus Heaney. He won the Nobel Prize for Literature a couple of years back. What McCourt does with his prose, Heaney does with verse."

Munro tossed the book back to her. "Another time," he said.

"You might have been born here, Agent Munro, but you have no concept of what it means to be from here. I'm not idly passing the time. I'm reminding myself how people like Cill Chainnigh think."

Again, Munro didn't speak but broadcast his emotions with his stare. The smile left her face, and she sighed heavily, standing up.

"All right, then," she said, "you're so eager. Let's get started."

Fisher walked into the kitchen so that she was a pace or two away from Kilkenny, where, when he raised his head, he would see her.

"Draw a glass of water and splash his face with it. Then, I want you to stand off to one side, so I'm the first person he sees," she said to Munro. "This is the protocol. I'm the interrogator. All his needs are met through me, and I decide which ones get met and when. Got that?"

"I've had the training," Munro replied.

She smiled at him. "Some of what you're about to see, they don't let you do. Get the water, please."

Munro felt his mouth go dry. As much as he wanted things to get moving, he was not looking forward to what was about to happen. It was risky. Too little threat and the subject laughed at you. Too much and you risked the subject's death or unbreakable stubbornness. It took at expert at causing pain to know the correct amplitude of discomfort, and apparently Mai Fisher fit that role. He found that realization both excited and unnerved him.

Munro walked stiffly to the sink and filled a glass with cold water from the tap. He moved to Kilkenny's right side and looked over at Fisher. He had seen some compassion come to her face when he told his story. Now, she was bereft of emotion again. She gave him a nod. Munro's arm moved swiftly. The water hit Kilkenny directly in the face, some entering his open mouth. He sputtered, coughed, and blinked his eyes open.

"Look at me," Fisher commanded.

Kilkenny blinked again and studied her with bloodshot eyes. The spread of his smile was slow as recognition grew.

"Well, well," he said. "It's herself, then." Munro watched Kilkenny's eyes glide up and down Fisher's frame. "You look pretty good for a corpse," he said. "Much better than the others you betrayed. Bits and pieces they were."

Fisher didn't reply, merely watched Kilkenny, her face expressionless.

"That was cold-blooded, you know," Kilkenny went on. "Tell me. Did you fuck young Declan the night before you killed him?"

"No," she replied, quietly. "I did that the morning of."

Fisher said something to Kilkenny, and Munro didn't recognize the language. Something guttural. Kilkenny answered in the same language.

"What did you say?" Munro said. Fisher cut him a warning look.

Kilkenny turned his head toward Munro's voice. "Ah, that would be the loving da."

While Kilkenny's head was turned, Mai closed the distance between them and punched him on the left temple then in the nose, two quick jabs that raised a mouse next to his eye and sent blood streaming over his lips. Kilkenny glanced again at Munro, seeking his reaction.

His own words dying on his lips, Munro remembered the protocol and let Mai speak.

"We're not doing 'good cop, bad cop,' Eamon," Fisher said. "Don't look to him. I'm the one you should be worrying about."

Kilkenny looked back at her and smiled, blood staining his teeth. In that strange language again he said something, and this time Fisher punched him in the stomach. She quickly stepped back as Kilkenny spewed vomit. Munro found himself rooted as he watched what happened next. Fisher punched Kilkenny in the stomach and face until she opened the skin of one of her knuckles on his cheekbone. Only then did she step back, panting slightly, and move to the kitchen sink, where she began to run cold water over her hand.

Munro could hear Kilkenny's ragged breathing and could see the swelling already beginning in his face. He walked up to Fisher, leaned close and whispered to her.

"What the fuck are you doing?" he demanded.

"Beating the crap of the bastard who has your daughter," she replied, her eyes issuing Munro another warning.

He ignored it. "The point is to get him to talk. Not beat him senseless."

"Munro, we agreed about this. Don't get prissy cop on me now. Besides he's not the type of person we can reason with. You cannot appeal to his good side because he has none." She held up her bruised hand, clenched in a fist. "This is one thing he understands," she said. She lowered that hand and reached behind her back, withdrawing a Beretta 92F. "This is another."

Before Munro could protest, she walked back to Kilkenny.

"All right, Eamon, as you may have noticed, things are not going to go exactly as you planned," she said.

"Aren't they, girl?" he asked.

"I'll start by shooting off your toes, one by one, then kneecaps, elbows, work my way up."

"And spare me prick?" he grinned.

In Gaelic, she said, "I thought I'd leave that for the father of the girl you kidnapped."

"You're a smart woman," was the reply, also in Gaelic. "You must have figured it out."

"Is she buried alive somewhere, slowly running out of oxygen?"

"No. You set the example 13 years ago, girl. Think about that."

"English!" Munro shouted.

Fisher's expression for him was dangerous. "I will only warn you once," she said to Munro. "Shut up."

"I have a right to know what you're talking about," Munro said. "And there will be no shooting."

"No stomach for it, do you?" Kilkenny tossed over his shoulder to him. "She can beat me all she wants. She can shoot every digit off my body. I won't talk." He looked back at Fisher and switched to Gaelic again. "I won't talk until you finish it. You know what I'm talking about. I'm a dead man anyway. Cancer. Four or five months to go, and that's a year longer than I was told to begin with. I'm not going to die until you do, but that young girl will die first. Just like all those people, your friends, did 13 years ago. But you can stop it right now."

Munro had no idea what was being said. His world was Fisher's emotionless face and Kilkenny's obvious rage. He watched the Irishman look at the gun in Fisher's hand then look at her. And Munro knew.

"Mai," he said. "We need to talk."

"Not now, Munro."

"Yes, now."

"It's worried about his daughter, he is," said Kilkenny. Fisher smashed the butt of the Beretta against Kilkenny's chin.

"Mai!" Munro said, and she finally looked at him to see his Sig Sauer pointed at her. Her look was incredulous. "We talk now."

The struggle was acute, but she holstered her Beretta and strode away to the front of the house not bothering to see if Munro followed her. When he entered the sitting room, she turned to him and smiled.

"I think that's going well," she said.

"He wants you to kill yourself," Munro said.

"No shit, Munro. All those years in the Secret Service. You're a credit to them."

"Cut the sarcasm. Don't lose sight of what we're doing here."

"What is it I've lost sight of?"

"You're letting him bait you."

"I'm letting him think he's baiting me, and you're interfering." Munro frowned, and she paced impatiently. "It's given that he wants me dead, but he wants to make a statement. He wants me to kill myself because I've caused your daughter to die."

Munro looked away. "Do not play this game with my daughter's life," he said.

"It's not my game, Munro. It's Cill Chainnigh's. He wants me to lose it totally and kill him before he tells us where Deidre is. He wants another one on my conscience. He will never talk, Munro. You've got to understand that. He's not going to tell us, no matter what I do to him or to myself." She stopped pacing, standing next to him, her hand on his arm. "I'm sorry, Munro. Your daughter's probably dead. She's probably been dead since you arranged the meet."

"Jesus, Jesus," Munro said, pressing the heels of his hands to his temples and walking away from her.

"I'm sorry," Mai said again. "I really am, but I'm certainly not going to give him the satisfaction of blowing my brains out in front of him."

Munro wanted her to shut up, wanted to smash his fist in her face as she had done to Kilkenny. He needed to think. Kilkenny was willing to let her beat him to a pulp, mutilate him, and not give her what she wanted. She knew that, and now Munro knew it, but Kilkenny didn't know that Munro knew it. Munro inhaled a deep breath, reached inside, and found his resolve. When he looked up at Fisher again, he saw her momentarily taken back then she was curious.

"It's now time for 'good cop, bad cop,'" he said, and he saw her consider.

*   *   *

The toll of the beating he had received was on every inch of Kilkenny's face when Munro came back into the kitchen. Munro went to the sink to draw the man some water, but he saw Fisher rudely smack the side of Kilkenny's head as she walked behind him.

"Ah," Kilkenny sighed, "the return of your tender ministrations, Maggie. I like that name better, Maggie, a sweet name," he crooned. "Margaret O Mailligh. Young Declan was in love with Maggie O Mailligh, you know. He would have done anything for you, even die, which he did, didn't he?"

"Who told you who I was?" Fisher asked quietly.

"Well, I'll give you that one," Kilkenny said, smiling. "An RUC corporal's conscience got the better of him a couple of years ago, and he decided he needed to do something for the Cause. He told me."

"Did you kidnap his child as well?"

Kilkenny wheezed a laugh. "No, no. He gave it up for free."

"What is his name?"

Kilkenny laughed again. "I killed him. I didn't want his conscience reversing on me."

"I'll not be taking your word on that. His name."

With a shrug, Kilkenny told her. She looked up at Munro, who stood nearby with a glass of water in his hand. Kilkenny followed her glance.

"Is that for me, then?" he asked. "God, my throat is dry."

"That's not for him," Fisher told Munro.

"How can the man talk, for God's sake, if we don't give him water?" Munro said.

"How can you even think of giving water to the man who kidnapped your daughter?"

"I'll give him my fucking house if he'll just tell me where she is."

"Well, now," Kilkenny interjected. "That sounds like a man who can be dealt with. Not like you, my girl. Batting those eyes, getting us all believing you were one of us, when all along you were just another fucking traitor."

Fisher took a step toward him, but Munro interceded. "We agreed there would be no more of that," Munro said.

Fisher's index finger was in his face. "Then, your daughter's life is on you," she said, "because I can make this piece of shit talk."

"You're nothing but a whore," Kilkenny said in Gaelic. "Striapach," he spat. "Who paid you to kill your friends, the people who trusted you? Do you sleep at night knowing you betrayed them?"

Fisher shoved Munro aside, grabbed a fistful of Kilkenny's undershirt, and began to pound him again. Munro recovered and pulled her off, but she lunged at Kilkenny. Munro shoved her backwards, sending her nearly to her knees. She straightened and back-handed him, starting a bubble of blood in Munro's nostril. She went back to Kilkenny.

"Tell me where Deidre Munro is," Mai demanded, punctuating each word with a fist to his already pulpy face. Munro pulled her off yet again, this time reaching from behind and grabbing her wrists. She struggled against Munro, who was stronger, but he had her under his control.

"Ah," Kilkenny sighed, "it's been too long since that happened." His voice was slurred through his swollen lips. He stared down at his lap.

Munro heard Fisher's curse. Her beating had given Kilkenny quite the erection. The head of his blue-veined penis had pushed through the flap of his baggy boxer shorts.

"Thank you, girl," he sneered and began to laugh.

"That's it," Munro said, still holding Fisher by her wrists and pushing her ahead of him. "You're done." He pushed her down the hallway to the front room and shoved her inside. "Come out of here," he told her, "and I'll fucking kill you."

*   *   *

Suddenly weary from dealing with the ghosts disturbed by Cill Chainnigh, Mai sat in an arm chair, her head back, her eyes closed. That bright November morning came back to her, when she and Declan Muineachan returned from a perimeter patrol and found everyone at their morning meal instead of out about the farm. Cill Chainnigh had been adamant that no one be idle, and the farm was kept working. That particular morning everyone was lazy, knowing Cill Chainnigh, having delivered the Semtex, wouldn't be back for a while. That they were all so casual and lazy had disturbed Mai, and she remembered she had checked her watch and thought there were a good 15 minutes left.

But something had kept her from entering the house. Some telltale or her intuition, she'd never been able to remember. What she did recall was that she called out no warning to anyone, not even Declan, on his way inside for a "cuppa tea." He had turned into the doorway and smiled at her, a smile of promise and love that was wiped away in an instant.

Thirteen years ago—she glanced at her watch—20 minutes from now.

Straightening in the chair, she took a cell phone from her pocket, flipped it open, and dialed a number. The person who answered spoke

Russian, and she replied in kind, her words precise, none superfluous, none questioned. When she was done, she sat back and waited.

⋆　　　⋆　　　⋆

Munro retrieved the glass of water he had set aside and held it to Kilkenny's distended lips. Sloppily, the man gulped it down, some of it dribbling over his lips and down the front of the undershirt stained with blood. Keeping the distaste off his face, Munro saw that the man's erection was still prominent.

"Ah," Kilkenny sighed, "all I need is a wee rest. Bring her back, then."

Munro calmly walked back to the sink, setting the glass down. He braced both hands on the worn counter and lowered his head. Images of Deidre—her fifth birthday party, her first Communion, high school graduation, waving to him as she had boarded the plane for Ireland weeks ago—assaulted him, threatened to unman him. There was an emptiness in him, the void of a parent who has lost a child. Munro inhaled deeply, calling upon his will. The void filled with his need for retribution. Munro picked up a twin of the chair Kilkenny sat in and walked to the man. Munro placed the chair with its back facing Kilkenny and straddled it. He studied the pulpy face. Never before had he experienced anything like this. He had participated in the interrogation of the occasional counterfeiter, an odd nut case or two who had written a threatening letter to the President or First Lady. They were very controlled situations, sometimes with lawyers present. No threats, except of prosecution. Just carefully designed questioning. Certainly nothing involving the shedding of blood by beating a man senseless or what Munro was now about to do. Munro bent down and retrieved his back-up gun from an ankle holster, a snub-nose, five-shot Smith and Wesson revolver.

"Where's the lass, then?" Kilkenny asked. "Maggie, that is."

Munro couldn't look at Kilkenny. If he did he would lose his resolve.

"She's not coming back," he said.

"That was our deal. Bring her back."

Munro thumbed the cylinder release on the Smith, pushed the cylinder clear of the revolver's body, depressed the plunger, and dumped the five hollow-point rounds into his palm. He re-loaded one into a chamber and pocketed the other four.

"Here, then," Kilkenny said, some bravura gone. "I said, this is not what we agreed to. I'll deal only with her."

The pounding of his blood in Munro's ears muffling Kilkenny's words, Munro spun the cylinder and snapped it shut without looking at it. His gaze fell on Kilkenny's lap, and Munro couldn't help but smile. He'd known some fellow agents who got boners from handling their guns. Kilkenny had lost his watching Munro's S&W being pointed at his head.

"You deal with me, now," Munro said.

"Now, then," Kilkenny tried, with a feeble smile, "if you kill me, you won't find your daughter."

"Then tell me where she is."

"The bitch. I'll only tell her."

"She's not a player anymore. It's just you and me. You've got until the count of three."

"It's a real cowboy you are, then."

"One."

"You won't do it. You won't risk your daughter's life."

"Two." Though the Smith revolver could be fired double action, Munro cocked the hammer, its sound having an effect.

"You're not like her." Kilkenny jerked his head toward where Munro had taken Fisher. "She's the user, not you. She sacrificed nine people because a government paid her to. You won't sacrifice your daughter's…"

"Three."

Munro pulled the trigger, and the hammer fell on an empty chamber. The acrid stench of urine met his nose. He cocked the hammer again.

"Let's see if you'll shit yourself this time," Munro said. He finally met Kilkenny's eyes and found his own fear reflected in them.

"Hail Mary, full of grace," began Kilkenny.

"One."

"The Lord is with thee. Blessed art thou among women."

"Two."

"And blessed is the fruit of thy womb, Jesus. Holy Mary…"

"Mother of God," Munro said, "Pray for us sinners now and at the hour of our death." He paused. "Three."

Kilkenny began to weep and mutter the Hail Mary again after the hammer closed on another empty chamber. Again, Munro cocked the hammer.

"One."

Kilkenny's voice muttered on, different words this time. No prayer, no supplication. He gave Munro exactly what he wanted.

*　　　*　　　*

Munro walked into the sitting room and sat heavily on a chair across from Mai. She studied his face and felt her throat tighten with emotion.

"She was in what was left of the basement of that farmhouse in Lifford," he murmured to her. "Wired to a bomb." Mai only nodded. "I loved her more than my life."

Mai got up from her chair and crossed to him. She knelt down and slipped the revolver she had spotted from its ankle holster then tossed it on the other chair. Straightening, she slid a hand under his jacket, took the Sig Sauer out of a shoulder holster, and tossed it to join the Smith. Munro caught her wrists, pulled her onto his lap, straddling him, and crushed his mouth against hers. His hands spanned her waist, gliding under the sweater she wore to trail heat along her back. His kisses were insistent and probing, and Mai put her hands on either side of his face, letting him kiss her. Her response was minimal, and she knew he would soon catch himself. Undeterred, his fingers fumbled with her bra, searching futilely for the clasp. There was a certain character of the chastity belt about a sports bra.

Mai pulled her face away from his. "Munro," she whispered.

"My mother used to call me Liam," he murmured. "My Irish name." He moved to close his mouth on hers again.

"Munro," she repeated, then her cell phone rang, startling them both. Munro released her, and she stood, bringing the phone to her ear.

*   *   *

Munro shook his head, felt his hands tremble, his body cool when it lost contact with Fisher's. His daughter lay dead, blown up by a terrorist's bomb, and he had been thinking below his belt.

"Da?" he heard Fisher say. Russian. "Da," she said again, then a rapid string of words. When Munro looked up at her, she was smiling.

*   *   *

A Coleman lantern was the only illumination in the crater. The shadows were deep and frightening, but the pool of incandescent light showed enough detail that she knew she was in what had been a basement. What had happened to the house above, there was no way to tell.

For days, she had tried to be what her father would expect her to be, calm and brave, trusting him to do what he needed to do to get her out of this. In the past he had always used adverse situations to teach a lesson, standing to the side and guiding her through self-extrication. Her childhood scrapes had never been anything like this. Sitting tied up on the dank floor of an earthen basement wearing a vest full of plastic explosives was not exactly something her father had been able to teach her how to deal with.

Oddly enough, she was no longer afraid of dying from the explosion. That would be quick. Alive one second, not the next. What bothered her was the look her guard kept giving her. He had undressed her a hundred times with his eyes, and she was angry that she had been unsuccessful in keeping a reaction off her face. That amused him, made his leer deeper, more personal. She was glad she'd given up her virginity years ago on the night of the Junior/Senior Prom. Christ, would her Dad shit if he knew that. If this asshole was going to rape her before she died, at least he wouldn't get the satisfaction of raping a virgin. She had already decided, if it happened, she was going to pretend to enjoy it. Rape was power, after all, and not sex.

Between leering at her and smoking cigarettes, the guard had constantly checked his watch, then finally stubbed out a half-smoked cigarette. He walked over to her and set a timer on the explosives strapped to her chest. She had closed her eyes as his hands caressed her, and she did hide a triumphant smile when he stopped as she moaned in pleasure. He had smacked her, called her a striapach, a whore. She'd learned enough Gaelic to know that word. Then he backed away, resuming his seat on the pile of rubble. He lit another cigarette and began to check his watch again. With a sinking heart, she realized he was going to wait until the last minute then go, leaving her with the knowledge there would be no time for him to return and stop the timer, with the knowledge that her father wouldn't arrive in time either.

He would have tried. She knew that. Her father's love was unconditional. She used to tease him about that, told him it was his guilt at being a single parent. He would look wounded until he realized she was joking. Profound sadness nearly made her cry, and she realized her pain would be over quickly. Her father's would go on forever. She sent a little prayer to him, asking him not to mourn too long, and tried to relax.

Her guard lit another cigarette, checked his watch yet again, and gave her a smile. She struggled not to lower her head and look at the timer, but, even now, her curiosity got the best of her. Three minutes. Three minutes to live. Christ, she thought. My Daddy won't walk me down the aisle, won't hold his grandchildren. She couldn't stop the tears any longer and let them fall. She heard her guard chuckle, and she looked up at him, communicating as much spite as she could.

The chuckle stopped, the cigarette slipped from his fingers, and his eyes widened in surprise. I must really have the evil eye, she thought. Then, his whole body relaxed, melting to the dirt floor, that expression of surprise etched on his features. Behind where he had sat stood a second man, holding a bloody knife. His narrowed eyes studied her, even as he bent down and carefully cleaned the knife on the dead man's clothes. The newcomer began to approach her, and she looked down at the timer again. One minute and 25 seconds. The tears began in earnest. The man knelt in front of her. His face was harsh, his crew cut making him seem almost bald.

"Shh, shh," he soothed. "Patience." He studied the arrangement strapped to her chest and made a sound of contempt. "Amateurs," he muttered, his fingers moving swiftly over the vest.

In her head the timer was ticking down, and her breath began to quicken.

"Oh, God," she whispered, "Oh, God, oh God, oh God."

"Shh," the man said again. "Is all right. No problem."

She opened her eyes wide. "No problem? No fucking problem?" she shouted at him.

He rocked back on his heels and smiled at her, pointing to her chest. Puzzled, she looked down. The timer had frozen at 22 seconds. All right, now I'm going to get hysterical, she thought, and began to cry in heaving sobs.

The man pulled the vest off her, untied her hands, then covered her with his own coat, all the while soothing her and speaking a language she didn't understand. Finally, she managed to swallow the sobs and look at him. He smiled at her and gently dried her face with his fingers.

"Better now?" he asked. Not trusting herself to keep from crying again, she nodded. "Okay," he said, "just relax a minute more."

He took a cell phone from his trouser pocket and punched in a number. Someone must have answered instantly because he began to speak in that strange language again, then he held the phone toward her. She stared at it then looked at her rescuer. He continued to smile and nodded at her.

"Uhtyets," he said, then remembered English. "Father."

Her fingers trembling, she took the phone and murmured, "Daddy?"

*   *   *

When Munro looked up at her, she was smiling.

"It's for you," Mai said.

"What?"

Fisher held out the phone to him, and he took it, bringing it to his ear. "Munro here," he said.

A voice he never expected to hear again spoke to him, and he no longer cared whom he was with. He wept, Deidre wept, and when he looked again at Mai Fisher, he saw her eyes were moist. The conversation was all too brief, and Fisher took the phone back to speak again in Russian. Munro sat back in his chair, exhausted and exhilarated, a dream quality to everything around him. Fisher broke the connection and dialed another number.

"I'm leaving my cousin's home," he heard her say, "please arrange for a trash pick-up as soon as possible." Then she rang off again. In a moment, Munro felt her hand on his shoulder. "Munro, go on out to the car."

He blinked and looked up at her. She was so attractive, her features no longer hard and angry as they had been with Kilkenny. Munro remembered the kisses and felt the heat from her hand.

"Go on out to the car," she urged again. "I'll make a last sweep in here, then we'll be on our way to Deidre."

That he understood. Munro placed his hand over hers and stood, still holding it. He bent down and kissed her again, and this time she truly reacted to it. Turning from her before it got out of hand, he walked out the front door of the safe house toward the car. The sun made him squint. He had no idea it was morning.

*   *   *

Mai walked through the house, making sure they had left nothing behind. Once they were gone, the house would be "swept," removing any fingerprints, fibers, hairs they had deposited, but she searched for obvious items—gloves, their coats, a muffler Munro had worn around his neck. She saved the kitchen for last.

She stood for several moments looking down at Cill Chainnigh, studying the bald spot on his crown. He seemed much smaller and far less dangerous than she had remembered him, no longer a threat to husbands and fathers, brothers and sisters, wives and mothers, or children.

Thirteen years before she had killed nine people at Lifford to save hundreds. The final actor in that play sat here before her, dead at last, as he should have been 13 years ago. Declan Muineachan was the one who should have lived to bounce his children on his knees, she thought. Cill Chainnigh should have died at Lifford, and so should have she.

She turned her back on all of it and walked to the car.

*   *   *

By using her private plane, Mai and Munro actually beat Kolya and Deidre to Belfast, site of the Maitland family home. The reunion was everything to be hoped for, even making Kolya's cheeks flush with emotion and forcing him to mutter something about patrolling the grounds, just in case. A doctor was out of the question because that would mean involving the authorities, but a hot bath and her father's shoulders to cry on had done wonders for Deidre Munro. For her own healing, Mai opted for the British cure-all: She boiled water and fixed a strong pot of tea but opened a good bottle of Merlot for later. Wine really mellowed her, and she decided it was best that Kolya and Deidre were chaperones. It had been a long time since she had been sexually tempted by anyone other than Alexei.

Munro, with a significant five o'clock shadow that made him additionally appealing, came into the kitchen of the old house and seemed surprised to see her sitting at a weathered wooden table and nursing her tea.

"Asleep?" Mai asked.

"Yeah," he replied, dry washing his face. He looked at the tea then saw the bottle of wine with two glasses sitting beside it. "Do you mind if I start with that?" he said pointing to the Merlot.

"You need it," Mai answered. "Go ahead."

After he had poured himself a generous amount, he joined her at the table, at first moving to the chair beside her then moving to the one across from her. Mai smiled slightly. She wasn't the only one feeling temptation.

"How is she doing?" Mai asked.

"Better than expected. Just some bruises. No, ah," he blushed a bit and drank a good swallow of wine, "no rape."

"I'm glad. Sometimes that's a given, but I'm glad Cill Chainnigh was focused on another agenda."

"Speaking of agendas, I've been doing some thinking," Munro said.

"You have been quiet."

"I think you figured this out a long time ago."

"Why do you think that?"

"Your Russian appendage was too conveniently close."

"Are you complaining?"

"No, no. Just wondering if I've been used. If my daughter has been used."

She studied his face and read the suspicion there.

"Let's see," she mused. "My 'Russian appendage' just saved your daughter's life, and you have the balls to ask me if I wanted Eamon Cill Chainnigh enough to use you and your daughter?"

Munro returned her stare in a way that made her realize he did have the balls.

"I am a user, Munro," she conceded. "That ability is a valuable tool in my business, but I don't casually toy with people's lives, especially innocent ones." His eyes asked again his original question, and she wondered why she felt compelled to answer. "Yes, I figured it out."

"When?"

"In the lounge of the Hay-Adams."

"Fuck you."

"You did have that on your mind earlier. Look, I knew Cill Chainnigh, and as soon as you told me the story I knew what he was after. It was only logical that he would take your daughter to the place where my 'crime' was committed, so I could commit another one there by proxy. What we couldn't afford to do was move too fast, which you would have wanted to do if I had told you."

"You used us."

She sighed and set her cup down. "I can see how it seems that way to you. If we had moved too early, Deidre would be dead."

"You don't know that."

"I do know it, Munro. I know it because if the situation were reversed, if I had needed to use something or someone to get to Cill Chainnigh, I would have done the same thing he did."

Munro shook his head, as if denying her words. "What you knew was that her life was in the balance, and you went ahead."

"It never ceases to amaze me that people are surprised at this: I work in a business where I manipulate people on a daily basis in the pursuit of a sometimes vague agenda called peace and national security. Sometimes I fuck up badly. More often I save lives. From the beginning I had this one under control, and your daughter lies upstairs sleeping. You'll get to take her home, Munro, and I'm glad I was able to give that to you. If you want to be angry at me for the methodology, that's all right. I respect you too much to be bothered by that anger."

His eyes were completely disbelieving. "You respect me? That is not something I would have expected."

"I don't give my respect easily and certainly not to Feds."

Munro relented and smiled slightly at that.

"Munro," she said, after they drank a while in silence, "you killed Cill Chainnigh."

He drank off his wine and stared back at her. "Maybe he died of your beating," he replied.

Christ, he'd be good at espionage, so dissembling was that answer, she thought. Mai stared at him a long time, communicating what she knew. "Maybe," she said.

But not likely. When she'd entered the kitchen to do the preliminary sweep, she saw that Cill Chainnigh's neck had been broken. That was part of the respect she owned Munro, the part she couldn't articulate because she hated it when she was patronized. Munro had killed Cill Chainnigh because Munro didn't want another casualty of Lifford on her conscience. He didn't know her well enough to understand her overburdened conscience didn't care one way or another how many more it took on.

"By the way," she said. "I'm sorry for hitting you. It was one of the hardest things I've ever had to do."

"Smacking me upside the head?"

"No," she explained, smiling at him, "holding back from knocking you out so I could kill Cill Chainnigh myself."

His surprise was only momentary, then he laughed, toasting her with his empty glass as he got up to refill it. Mai poured another cup of tea from the pot and thought how easy it was to respect Munro for killing Cill Chainnigh when her long list of victims left her with so little respect for herself. Like she, he had been weak and given into his baser impulses, but he had only beaten her to it. She had wanted to kill Cill Chainnigh merely because he was there, because he was whom he was, because he hadn't died at Lifford. Munro's motivations were far nobler, and that made him strong—just like the husband who was now not so distant and less difficult than she believed. She would leave Kolya here with Munro and Deidre and take her plane to The Hague for a reunion of her own that was long overdue. The unhesitant grappling with Munro had shown her that.

With some regret for her faithfulness, Mai glanced at Munro, who stood at the doorway of the kitchen looking out over the house's flower garden, meticulously kept though no one lived here. At some point, she thought, she could use William Henry Munro again in her business, but what she would tell him was that he was a useful ally, someone to have at your back.

But only sometimes.

For Better or Worse

◆

So intense was the dream that when he woke, he reached to his right as he had thousands of times, expecting his hand to touch a familiar form. His questing fingers encountered only the cool, smooth, flat expanse of the coverlet. In disappointment he rolled onto his back, still clutching where he had dreamed she was lying. He stared at the ceiling, lost somewhere in the darkness above him, and tried to will himself back to sleep, but it wouldn't come. Finally, he gave up and sat on the side of the bed, dry-washing his face with his hands. He switched on the lamp by the bed and read the clock. Three-fifteen. Another night with four hours sleep. The irony was inescapable: He had taken a desk job to get more rest. Somehow, it wasn't working out as he'd planned.

In fact, nothing was working out as he expected. The desk job, though important and meaningful work, was tedious and boring, and he was doing the job alone. He lived in a rented house in The Hague and worked for the UN at the World Court, specifically, for the War Crimes Tribunal for Bosnia-Herzegovina. His partner of 20 years, who was also his lover, his best friend, and his wife, worked for the UN, too, but for its intelligence gathering organization. She was living God knew where, in a tent or a barracks in Serbia or Croatia or Bosnia, or maybe, if the need arose, in Belfast. If none of those places harbored her, then she could be in their house in America, outside of Washington, DC. He simply had no way of knowing. He hadn't spoken to her in weeks, and as prideful as she was, he had his pride, too. All too often during one of their disputes, it had been he who relented first and went crawling back to her. Not this time. This time, she'd have to do the crawling.

"Right, Bukharin," he muttered to himself, "and how likely is that to happen?"

He stood up and padded in his bare feet into the kitchen and turned on the coffee he'd set up the night before—only a few hours ago, really. He was awake, and it wouldn't hurt to get to the office early and be the consultant that he was to the War Crimes Tribunal. That consisted largely of sitting in a court room day after day, listening to gut-wrenching testimony by witnesses and victims and mendacious denials by the accused and occasionally being asked a question of clarification by the judges or the prosecution. The necessity of the work he would never deny. He just never realized it would be so incredibly monotonous.

Just as monotonous as watching the brewing coffee drip into the carafe. He reached for the phone on the kitchen wall and dialed a cell phone number from memory. The time delay was only a few seconds as the signal routed among several satellites. There were three rings before a computer voice answered.

"The satellite customer you are trying to reach is either outside the service area or has turned off the instrument. Please try again later. Thank you. Message 4507."

The temptation to slam the receiver back onto its cradle was strong, but he resisted it, instead going to the dish drainer and taking up his coffee cup. It was battered and chipped, but his granddaughter had made it for him when she was 10 and had taken a pottery class his wife, Mai, had enrolled her in. She had made Mai one as well, and idly Alexei wondered where that cup was. As he sipped black coffee and stared out the window into the darkness, he realized he had nothing in this place that was a memento of his wife. He had selected and rented it hoping she would relent and join him, but she had never set foot in it. No detritus of her was anywhere to be found, no cast-off underwear, no lipstick or earring left behind. Nothing to show that he'd been married to her for nearly 21 years, that he loved her and missed her desperately.

Alexei Nicholeivitch Bukharin, former spy turned bureaucrat, drained his first cup of coffee, poured himself a second, and went to his computer. Since he was awake there was no reason not to get some work done.

*   *   *

The morning recess was a welcome break for everyone in the courtroom. A succession of women—from grandmothers to those almost impossibly young for the horror inflicted upon them—had testified, describing in excruciating detail their rapes and pointing out their rapist, a baby-faced young man sitting behind the defense table. His face may have spoken innocence, but the smirk on his face bespoke his guilt. He openly sneered at the witness, turning at one point to his lawyer and speaking loudly enough for Alexei to hear him say, "They can't possibly believe I'd put it in that dog." Alexei had resisted the temptation to stride across the courtroom and smash the bastard's face in.

The tribunal of judges had listened stoically to the witnesses, though the chief judge, an American woman who was a respected jurist, struggled with her neutrality, Alexei noted. The two of them had shared many a brandy in her chambers after court, and he had listened, allowing her to vent. They had become good friends, but nothing more, since she was happily married. She, too, was a good listener, and had been the only one Alexei could speak to of his loneliness and sense of failure.

During the recess he reviewed transcripts of previous testimony to highlight salient points for the prosecutors. He sat in the commissary of the World Court, drinking more coffee. He'd been drinking entirely too much of it lately, as his latest physical had indicated when the doctor admonished him for an elevated blood pressure. Nothing serious or abnormal. Just outside his normal range. When the doctor had asked if anything unusual was going on in his life to cause the problem, Alexei had nearly laughed. Nothing at all unusual, doctor, he had thought. I sit day after day and listen to the most horrific accounts of torture, rape, and murder—some of which I personally witnessed, by the way, and was unable to prevent—and my wife prefers to go spook around Eastern Europe instead of living with me. Just the average life of a retired spy.

He paused in his reading and took off the glasses he seemed to need a lot lately, rubbing his tired eyes. It had been out of concern for his partner that he had wanted to give up the action side of espionage. He was 15 years older than she, and, at 56, his reflexes and reactions had slowed. He had not wanted to be responsible for a misstep that would cost their lives. His wife, his partner, was still in her early 40's, and still addicted to the occasional excitement her work offered. Spurred by her need for justice, she would spy on anyone she was told to until she obtained the information she needed. At a time when he wanted to take fewer and fewer chances, she pushed for more. Their lives had come full circle, their role reversal complete.

At the age of 20 Alexei was a newly widowed Red Army soldier with an infant son whom he fostered to the child's maternal grandparents. Driven nearly insane by his grief, he'd become a top special forces operative then a KGB agent before he was given by the Soviet government to the United Nations Intelligence Team. He went from spying on his fellow countrymen to spying on whomever his director or the secretary-general wanted. For a long time his hope had been that someone would end his dark existence. Afraid of nothing and no one, he was a coward only when it came to taking his own life. Three and a half decades later he was still alive, along the way having acquired a new wife and a new reason to live.

Mai Fisher, his wife and partner, at the age of 19, had come to UNIT to fulfill her parents' legacy. They had been two of UNIT's earliest agents and casualties, killed by the Taiwanese after their cover as missionaries was blown by someone they trusted. Wealthy and somewhat spoiled, Mai approached espionage with a naïveté Alexei at first found endearing, even as he tried to train it out of her. Her approach, more or less successful until the winding down of the Cold War brought a no-holds-barred mentality to espionage, only served to twist her as her career continuously showed her the worst in humanity. Not that long ago, she was the one on the brink, convinced she had nothing to live for. In their years together, she had given him back his soul but lost hers in the process.

Still, he loved her. After so long not allowing himself to feel anything for anyone, he dropped his barriers and let her in. By the time he did, her feelings for him changed. So, their marriage had always been one where love was for the most part unrequited—first hers, now his. He was at the end of his career and wanted security and her companionship. She remained active in field work in the hopes she would die for a good cause, and he was powerless to change that.

The poster family for dysfunctional, he thought, checking his watch to see that he had another 40 minutes before court resumed. No more coffee, he told himself. Go for a walk, Alexei. Go to the gym, Alexei. Do something other than sit here and feel sorry for yourself. So, you're a nearly 60 year old former spy with a failed marriage. Not so different from most of the world. Get up. Do something.

He got up and purchased another cup of coffee then returned to his transcripts.

"Alexei?" someone asked from beside his right elbow, and he looked up into a pair of gray eyes. Gray eyes framed by a heart-shaped face, outlined by a nice mass of honey-blonde hair, atop a trim figure in a tan business suit. Legs that just did not end. Christ, he thought. I do not need this. Anne Hobard, scion of a New England family who boasted that they had been in America since the boat after the Mayflower, had been showing her obvious interest for several weeks. Accidental encounters after hours in the hallway outside Alexei's office, offers to have drinks, offers to have lunch, offers of much more that went unspoken. That he was sure of. Alexei could read that intent very clearly in women. It was a talent of his and a weakness. In the first third of his marriage, he had been unfaithful uncountable times, usually on purpose, but eventually had cemented his commitment to his wife and slipped only once since then. Despite the fact that his wife didn't live with him, he considered himself still very much married to her.

"Anne," he replied.

"Want some company?" she said with a deep smile. She was a damned good lawyer, Alexei knew from the background check he'd conducted before she joined the prosecutorial staff at the World Court. In the courtroom she was self-possessed and thoroughly in charge, her logical arguments irrefutable and her presentations captivating. In his private encounters with her, she insisted upon being a helpless twit, and he resented that she associated him with men who preferred that.

"Court resumes in just a few minutes," he replied. Just say no, Alexei, he chided himself.

"Not for a half hour. May I join you?" Her self-possession returned, and she sat down before he replied. "Are you all right? I noticed you rubbing your eyes. Do you need something for a headache? A neck massage perhaps?"

Right. A neck massage, which, if he agreed to, she'd likely administer right here in a commissary packed with acquaintances of his and his wife's.

"No, thanks," he replied. "Just old eyes."

She smiled. Perfect, white teeth, fixed by the best dentists in Boston, no doubt. "But nice ones," she said.

Oh, Christ, he thought again, but kept his face fixed in his practiced impassivity.

"Pretty harrowing this morning," she commented, daintily spearing some of her salad. Alexei wondered if she were eating so prissily because she thought it impressed him, then he decided he had entirely too much of his ego in the situation.

"Extremely," he replied.

"I don't usually go for the 'evil incarnate' routine," Anne said, "but when I look at that bastard, I really do think that some evil does walk around on two legs."

No quibbling with that, Alexei thought. "More often than not," he answered her.

"Alexei, I was wondering, well, I have two tickets to Ballet Russe in Amsterdam on Saturday," she began, "and I thought perhaps you might like to join me."

"Are you fond of ballet?" he asked, knowing perfectly well she wasn't. Her background had showed she abhorred the forced lessons she'd taken as a child.

"I just adore it."

"What are they performing?" he asked. He knew. The Director was an old Komsomol buddy of his who had already looked him up and treated him to dinner.

The self-assuredness fell again. She hadn't bothered to learn that and considered him shallow enough not to care. "I forgot," she murmured.

No, he thought, you assumed because I was Russian I'd be interested and that this was a way to show that we had mutual concerns.

"But the reviews were excellent," she added.

Actually the reviews had been tepid, which his old friend Misha had lamented over brandy. "There was something to be said about the old Soviet system, Alyosha," his friend had bemoaned, "at least it trained good dancers."

Anyone else, Alexei might have considered going simply because the two tickets were expensive. He knew, however, that though Anne's salary was commensurate with any public servant's, she had a substantial family income to fall back on. There were no qualms, then, about his decision.

"No, thanks."

"Why not?" she blurted, clearly surprised.

"It's inappropriate," he said.

"We work together, Alexei, but I don't work for you or you for me."

"That's not why it's inappropriate."

"The difference in ages doesn't bother me."

"Wrong again."

"I don't understand…"

"Anne, you know very well I'm married. To a woman, by the way, younger than I and with whom I've worked for more than 20 years."

"I know you're married, but I also know she left you."

"She didn't leave me," he retorted, hoping he didn't sound defensive. "I work here. She works elsewhere."

"That's not what I heard."

"Then, you place entirely too much credence in gossip. Quite frankly, I'm surprised. You're an intelligent and capable woman. I find it a bit disheartening that you listen to what people whisper in the bathroom stalls."

Alexei watched Anne study him pointedly. He had seen her make defendants squirm with that same expression, but it had little effect on him, except to make him notice that her mouth was generous and quite kissable.

"That was a bit defensive," she said.

"Not at all. Even if I were separated from my wife, that doesn't necessarily make me available."

"I was given to understand that didn't matter to you."

Damn the gossips anyway. Weren't people who worked for an espionage organization supposed to keep their mouths shut? Then, he remembered that technically he was retired from that organization and that the employees of the World Court had lips a bit looser than those of the United Nations Intelligence Team.

Time to be harsh. Calmly, he replied, "At one time it didn't, then it did, and it still does. I hope I'm clear on this. I have not sent you any signals that would imply that I'm interested in anything other than a profes-sional relationship with you, and you know it."

"Now's the time when you're supposed to say, 'Anne, you're a damned good lawyer.'"

"You are."

"A damned good and lonely lawyer. Just as lonely as you."

No one could be so lonely as I am, Alexei thought, but he said, "I hope not, Anne. There are plenty of men…"

"Shit, do not give me that line, either."

Alexei sighed. If he were the old Alexei, the one whose nickname was Ice, he could have pushed this woman and her feelings aside with-out compunction. That, or he would have taken her up on her offer before pushing her aside. Caring about people's feelings had definite disadvantages.

"Anne, my wife and I do different work right now, work that keeps us apart. Unlike some men who might view that as an opportunity to branch out, I'm not interested in replacing her in my heart or my bed. I won't apologize for feeling that way."

Anne had long since ceased eating her lunch and shoved the tray to one side. She leaned across the table toward Alexei. "And what will you do if she doesn't come back?" she asked.

Go after her, Alexei thought, but to Anne he made no reply. She got up regally, no emotion showing on her face either, collected her tray, and left.

I am a bastard, Alexei thought, but not for turning her down; for the fact that he turned and watched the sway of her hips as she walked away.

*   *   *

Because of the defense lawyer's incessant questioning of a witness after court resumed, the session had lasted until nearly seven in the evening. Then, the tribunal wanted all lawyers—prosecution and

defense—in chambers to discuss the treatment of one of the child witnesses by the defense. She had been 11 when raped and was nearly 16
now, but the defense lawyer was treating her as if the "alleged rape" had
occurred when she was at a sexually mature stage of her life instead of
in her childhood. There were bad feelings all around, and Alexei,
though he was not in the room, had been asked to observe the proceedings via surveillance camera.

The lead judge of the tribunal, the African-American woman jurist
Amelie Richardson, had comported herself well. Her finely chiseled face
communicated her rage at the defense tactics, though Alexei knew she
could be trusted to render impartial rulings. She would have also
admonished the prosecution for similar, distasteful tactics and had on a
number of occasions. Because Anne Hobard was part of the prosecution team, she was in the room, and Alexei found his eyes straying to her
repeatedly. She showed no sign of being affected by their encounter in
the commissary. Part of him admired her for that. The other part knew
that with self-possessed women as she, that calm could bespeak a storm
brewing beneath the surface. Keeping their encounters to an absolute
minimum was essential; so, when Judge Richardson had declared the
admonitions at an end, Alexei had beat a hasty retreat for home without
speaking to anyone.

Because he hadn't slept well the night before and because this had
been a long, tiring day, he wanted no more than to down a glass of wine
or two then go to bed and sleep through the night. As he walked from his
car to the front door of his rented house, he sorted the mail he'd picked
up from his box in the UN compound, hoping against hope that some
communication from his wife was there. No such luck. However, on one
envelope he recognized his granddaughter's familiar hand and was
bemused by that because she e-mailed him daily. Still, it was comforting
to touch something she had handled, and he tore open the envelope and
read the card. On the front was a familiar depiction of a kitten hanging
from a clothesline by its front paws. Inside were the words, "Hang in

there, baby." His granddaughter, Natalia, had written, "Papa, if I can get through exams, you can get through Mummy's being stubborn." Alexei smiled at the sentiment, though Natalia had probably sent Mai the same encouragement that she could outlast his intransigence.

The house he'd rented was in a part of the city where doctors, lawyers, and other elite lived. In fact Judge Richardson lived only two streets over, but Alexei's house backed onto the North Sea, and his patio atop the dike gave him a tremendous view. Many a warm night, he had slept with the windows open, the scent of the salt air helping him sleep. Tonight, when he entered the house, it was that smell of sea air that greeted him and made him stop in mid-motion, his hand hanging in the air before the light switch. He had not left a window or a door open. He was certain of that. His security consciousness would not have allowed it. Checking the doors and windows and setting the system was always the last thing he did before leaving in the mornings. Without a sound he set his briefcase against the wall beside the side door—Dutch houses were always entered from the side entrance—and lay his mail atop it. His right hand slipped under his jacket and emerged with his Walther P99. That was one part of his former life that he hadn't given up. He strained his ears for any sound. Faintly, the sounds of the waves met his ears. The normally pleasant resonance came from the rear of the house, where the French doors led to the seaside patio. That area was fenced in with a locked gate that opened to a set of stairs which led down to the beach. That was the only weakness in the security system, but he had wired extra sensors there. Whomever had gotten inside had done so by bypassing then resetting the system, one of his own design. It would take someone who knew him to…

Alexei felt his pulse begin to pound, and he inhaled deeply. Another scent mixed with the outside air. Chanel No. 5. He holstered the Walther and headed toward the rear of the house. In the kitchen on the ceramic tile counter, he saw an open bottle of red wine, approximately one glass of it missing and two empty wine glasses beside it, one with a faint hint of wine in the bottom of the bowl. Normally, he would have paused long enough to pour himself some. This time, however, he hurried past it, emerging from the open patio doors onto the stone patio itself. Empty except for the sturdy wrought iron furniture that had come with the place. The gate to the beach stairs yawned open, and he crossed to it. The stairs stretched down the dike 20 or so feet at about a 30-degree angle from the gate. At that point there was a small landing which offered a spectacular view of the North Sea. On the landing was a figure all in black so that she blended into the shadows of the night nearly upon them, but Alexei recognized her immediately. He knew every curve and indentation of her body, could feel them beneath his hands even when she was a thousand miles away. Inhaling a slight breath and holding it, he stopped, and she turned to him, her face a pale circle in the twilight. She smiled. Yes, she smiled. That was promising, and he tried to get his feet to move. They did so, reluctantly, not because he didn't want to be beside her but because he didn't want to appear over-eager.

When they were within reach of each other, she came to him, pressed against him as if she'd never been gone from his side, and Alexei first inhaled the scent of her—the French perfume, the sea air, the lavender shampoo and soap she used. Then, his mouth sought and found hers with a practice and ease of years of doing this same thing. Her mouth met his with enthusiasm, yielding to his search, her lips opening. Alexei tasted the red wine on her tongue. His hands moved freely, without seeking her permission, and hers were on him, too. Where their bodies touched there was warmth, and he hardly noticed the chill of the night. Finally, to take a deep breath, he moved his mouth from hers, but continued to give her light, tender kisses. He heard her throaty laughter, and it intensified his arousal. He kissed her again, then, Alexei felt her put her hands on either side of his face and free her mouth from his.

"Well," Mai Fisher murmured, "I missed you, too."

Did you, he thought, but kept his hands moving over her body, touching beneath her coat, assuring himself she was really here.

"I let myself in," she said.

"I noticed. You feel incredibly good."

"So do you. If you're going to continue rearranging my clothing, let's go inside."

"I'll stop. I just want to hold you."

"I don't want you to stop."

Alexei brushed tendrils of her hair back off her face and looked down into the familiar depths of her eyes, dark brown irises that sucked out your very soul, the round, Celtic face with its spattering of freckles. He had learned to love every character line he saw about those eyes, which were now bright with amusement and her own arousal.

"Are you really here?" he asked.

Her response was to kiss him deeply. "What does that feel like?"

"Like I'm going to embarrass myself in my pants if we don't get inside."

There came that laugh again as she eased away from him, taking his fingers in her hand and leading him back up the stairs.

*   *   *

The bedside light was low wattage. He had left it on because he wanted to be able to see her as he made love to her, and his concentration was totally on that and nothing else until they lay together afterwards, nestled against each other. Only then did his anger and resentment fight their way past his sexual satisfaction to enter his consciousness. Anger that she'd stayed away so long and with no communication. Resentment that she'd strolled into the house as if nothing had happened, as if he hadn't pleaded with her to be with him those months ago. And resentment that he'd been faced with Anne Hobard's lustful glances and assumptions because his wife hadn't been around. He had been married to Maitland Katherine Fisher for over 20 years, and it had always been a struggle to maintain, just as much when he was ordered to maintain it as when he wanted to maintain it. Instinctively, Alexei knew she wasn't back for good. This was a visit, a conjugal visit. She'd be here a few days until her lust was sated, then she'd be gone again. That was worth something, he supposed, that she didn't sate that lust with another man, and she would have had plenty of offers. Mai was an attractive woman whose sensuality was worn like clothing. Men either wanted her immediately or hated her arrogant feminism.

As attuned as he was to her moods and body language, she was just as synchronized to his.

"What is it?" she murmured, her lips at his ear.

"Nothing," he said.

"Every muscle in your body just tensed," she replied. "Are you upset?"

"Of course not, Mai. Every man doesn't see or hear from his wife for four months then she shows up as if nothing is wrong."

"But I notice that you waited until after sex to start The Argument." Her cultured English accent provided the emphasis.

She didn't move away from him, and he kept her in his embrace. Despite his anger, he wanted her flesh against his.

"I'm not starting The Argument," he replied. "I'm just upset with myself for thinking with my dick before any attempt at resolution. If you think I'm going to be content with your waltzing through The Hague every few months when you're horny, then think again."

"Well, I was horny," she replied after a moment's silence where he slowed his agitated breathing, "but that's not why I'm here."

"Why are you here?"

"Because I missed you, and I needed you, and I decided I had been stubborn enough. What I would like to do is spend a few days with each other with The Issue on the back burner, then talk about it reasonably."

"When was I unreasonable?"

"Let's see, could it have been, 'Mai, if you walk out that door you're walking out on me,' or was it, 'I've never known anyone more selfish and unfeeling than you?'"

"I think one's wife not wanting to live with one allows one some lack of reasonability."

"I never said I didn't want to live with you... Look, I don't want to talk about this now, and before you voice it, it's not because I want to avoid it. Alyosha, I just want to be with you, fall asleep with you, wake up with you, and enjoy this for a while before the acrimony resumes."

Alexei turned so that they faced each other, so that he could read her eyes. In the past few years that had become more and more difficult as she descended into a well of indifference. Right now her eyes showed neutrality, so the sincerity of her words was impossible to judge, but all the familiar and soothing features of her face were there, the ones he could close his eyes and bring to mind so easily.

"I love you," he said and saw emotion finally flicker on her face.

"I was beginning to worry," she said. "You hadn't told me."

"I will always love you, no matter what. You know that."

"Yes, I do, and that's rather unfair for you."

A smile played at his mouth. "Do I hear concern for another human being on those lips?" he asked.

"Sometimes I do wonder if any of your gender are worth it."

Alexei watched her face, marveling at how their intimacy beyond the physical resumed so easily. Tonight, at least, he could fall asleep in the same bed as she and wake up with that familiar face next to his on a pillow. When did that become so important to him? When did it lose its importance with Mai? One night, a dozen nights of peace would solve nothing if she left again. Not that long ago, he would have responded to her leaving with a revenge fuck, and that temptation was there since he had an all too willing candidate. One of them had to rise above all the dissention, and it might as well be he.

"I won't ask how long you're planning on staying," he said. "I'll just take what I can."

Emotion crossed her face again, more revealing than she'd been in years. Alexei saw guilt and regret but didn't dare think what that guilt and regret might be for. Certainly not for causing him any pain.

"I've fucked a lot of things up in my life," Mai said, "and mostly for the silliest of reasons. I am a tad on the uncompromising side."

"Really?" he said, smiling. "I hadn't noticed."

"At least you haven't lost your sense of humor," Mai replied. "I'm try-ing to tell you that I've overreacted to some things about your new job. I should have been more supportive and understanding, but I wasn't."

"That borders on an apology."

"So, it does. You could tone down the surprise, however. I've applied for a new job myself."

Alexei frowned. "What job? Where?"

"I'm getting to that. It seems that the local UNSECFOR commander is due for rotation back to his home country, and, well, I called in some markers."

It took him a moment to fathom it. "You're going to be the new UNSECFOR commander for the Tribunal?" he asked.

"Yes. A nine to five job for the most part. You will have to do your best to keep me from being bored."

"Are you doing this for me?" Alexei asked, knowing if that were true, resentment from her would soon follow.

"No. I'm doing it for us."

That admission had cost her a great deal of her precious independ-ence, Alexei knew. Mai had long since ceased thinking of them as "us," and he questioned why, all of a sudden, she was thinking that way again. There were a gamut of reasons from a near-death experience to… He kept the thought he was forming off his tongue and pushed it away. He couldn't handle the possibility that she had been with another man.

"Are you sure about this?" he asked.

"Yes. I start on Monday, so we have the weekend to make up for four months."

"I shall endeavor not to disappoint," he said, winking at her.

"And so will I," she murmured, easing into his embrace, her face against his chest so he couldn't see that she didn't share his amusement.

For better or worse, Alexei thought. Too bad we never vowed that because Mai always lives up to her word.

Her lips against his throat, she murmured, "You know, after four months, I would think that your recovery time would be shortened." Her hands descended below his waist.

"Keep doing what you're doing, and I might be able to overcome the ravages of my age," he replied, laying back and closing his eyes.

Her hands were gentle, deft, and the tone of her voice wicked. "I can do better than this," she said. Then, her mouth replaced her hands.

Days of Auld Lang Syne

———————— ◆ ————————

December 29, 1999

Munro felt as if he had a ton of grit beneath his eyelids. The recent long nights were not smart, he told himself. He needed to be alert, but last minute details had conspired to keep him not just awake at nights but at the "office." The office, in this case, was a temporary command center erected on the National Mall, basically a tent-like affair with separate "rooms," as well as the security nerve center itself. It was constructed of a special material that blocked attempts to listen in on any spoken or electronic communications conducted inside. Eavesdropping was the least of Munro's worries. The safety of tens of thousands of average citizens and hundreds of VIP's and the overlapping jurisdictions of more than a dozen federal and local law enforcement agencies were his primary concerns. The event that would bring them all together and cause his insomnia was a non-entity at least, a marketing scam at most.

By his own scientific reckoning, the true millennium was a year away, but Munro supposed that, despite the science fiction movie of that title which was a cultural icon, 2001 was not as sexy or marketable as "Y2K" or "MM." And if you weren't Christian, it wasn't really the millennium at all, just another year. Add in a good dose of paranoia about what would happen to certain aged computers when their internal clocks clicked over to a year ending in 00 and threats of internal and external terrorism that had been floating about for several years, Munro would be happy if the whole "America's Millennium" thing, the three-hour long entertainment extravaganza and fireworks display, were just called off. The mayor of Seattle, Washington, had Munro's admiration: In the face of several arrests of Arabs with fake passports and bomb-making ingredients in their cars attempting to cross from Canada into the U.S., Seattle's mayor had canceled the city's official celebration at the Space Needle. Why the Mayor of Washington, DC or the President didn't do the same, was a question Munro asked in silence. As head of security for the event, it was his job to make certain no one got hurt, not to question the decisions of bureaucrats and politicians.

Though the FBI had vied for the top slot, all security arrangements were being coordinated by the Secret Service. That was because the First Family would be in attendance, and that gave the Secret Service the ball to run with. Munro was selected to coordinate the effort because of his demonstrated ability and his seniority but also to acknowledge that he deserved the prestigious position as his swan song. After 25 years of serving five different Presidents, Munro was about to retire. Rather than accept this important job with the typical FIGMO—fuck it, got my orders—attitude, Munro approached it with his usual thoroughness and attention to detail. He had called in the best and brightest as assistant commanders, and he was surrounded by the elite of the Secret Service, FBI, ATF, Customs, DEA, Park Police, MPDC, Capitol Police, etc., ad infinitum. There was even a DC Public Housing Police—who knew? And each agent or officer was young enough to be his offspring. Among them were several attractive young women Munro would have considered asking out after his retirement, an ardor quickly quelled when one of them addressed him as "sir." How could you date someone who looked at you as if you were her father?

In fact one of them was speaking right now, giving the hourly update on street closings. She was dressed in tactical, black BDU's, and body armor, but Munro wasn't so old that he couldn't discern the curves. And they were nice ones. He sighed lightly. He felt like a dirty old man, lusting after one of his subordinates. His demeanor was all business, but he flushed slightly when he wondered what the woman agent would think if she could read his thoughts. Probably accuse him of sexual harassment. Ah well, just let me get through the next two days, and I can coast.

The agent concluded her report, and Munro thanked her. He checked his watch, hoping he could catch a nap before the next sitrep. He dismissed them all as he collated their written reports, then checked his watch again. Were UN reps always late for appointments? Or only this one? As if his thoughts had been read, a voice spoke behind him.

"She was rather attractive, wasn't she?"

Munro closed his eyes slightly, trying to keep a smile off his face. The cultured British accent was as he remembered it, as was its bearer's penchant for the dramatic. He stood up and turned toward the source of the voice. Fortyish, slim, dark brown hair pulled back in a clip at her neck, light makeup, the luminous brown eyes still the most striking feature. She was dressed in blue slacks, a dark blue turtleneck with a dark blue commando sweater over it. The slacks were neatly tucked into Lady Magnum assault boots, and she wore some subtle body armor as well. Holstered at her right side was a Beretta 92F, its grips betraying its longevity. Insignia on her turtleneck bore the initials UNSF, and the markings on her epaulets indicated the rank of Colonel.

"Don't you ever do things the usual way?" he asked.

She appeared thoughtful. "The 'usual way' is so boring," she replied. She pointed to the plastic ID badge clipped to her pistol belt. "I did check in and get the appropriate identification, though I saw about three ways I could have gotten past your security."

Careful, Munro, he told himself. She's baiting you. She likes to do that, remember?

"I hear you got a new job," he said.

"Well, yes. It keeps me from being the idle rich."

"Security chief for the Yugoslavian War Crimes Tribunal. You make it sound like nothing much."

"Compared to what I used to do, it is nothing much, but it means I'm with Alexei. That became important to me again."

"You miss your old life?"

"Let's see," she mused. "Do I miss skulking about, eavesdropping on people's lives, roughing up bad guys to get information out of them, getting slapped around, shot at, followed, threatened? You bet I do. We get an occasional spike of intrigue at The Hague, but mostly it's who's fucking whom."

"Do I detect bitterness?"

"Let's not go there, Munro."

"Okay." He pointed to her shoulders. "Do I have to call you 'Colonel?'"

"You do and I'll shoot you," she said, but she smiled. "When I switched from UNIT to UNSECFOR, the rank came along for the duration. Alexei says it gives me credibility." She shrugged. "Your message said you could use my help."

"You were supposed to be here two days ago."

"You know that I rarely jump at the command of the U.S. Federal government, but I'm here now. What's the specific threat that got the high-level request for my presence?"

"We've down-played it a lot, trying to keep the panic down, but we have a credible threat from a white supremacist group. They're coming to the Mall celebrations to kill all the interracial couples they see."

She nodded slightly. "You have a name?"

"Hopewell Reborn."

Munro thought Maitland Katherine Fisher paled somewhat, but that was the only manifestation, slight as it was, of any reaction to his words. She walked further into the room, glancing at the monitors and other equipment.

"It's not Elijah. He's dead," she commented, referring to the Christian Identity preacher she had old dealings with.

"It wasn't a man. A woman."

"Whom did she contact and how?"

"Me. By letter."

"How did she know to contact you?"

"My position as Coordinator was announced in the press."

"Do you have it? The letter?"

"We dusted it. No prints, or smeared prints. Not even a partial."

"No, I want to read it."

"I can get you a copy…"

"No, I want to see and read the original, and the envelope. Postmarked?"

"Idaho."

"Big surprise," she said, sarcastically. "How did you know it was a woman?"

"She signed the letter, 'Sarai, Aryan Mother.'"

"Interesting that it would be a woman. Elijah had a very distinct opinion of the role of women, and heading up a rebirth of Hopewell was not one of them. You know, you really needed Alexei here, not I. He was the one on the inside of the original Hopewell."

"He didn't come with you?"

Her smile was coy, not a word he would normally use to describe her, but coy she was. "Why? Afraid you won't have me all to yourself?"

Munro smiled back just as coyly. "Maybe I just wanted an excuse to see you again."

"I saw the way you were looking at that agent while she gave her report."

Munro winced. "That obvious?"

"To an astute observer of human nature. And the answer is no. Alexei is still in The Hague, noting, by the way, that the request was for my services."

Frowning Munro asked. "How much does he know about, ah, when we, ah, worked together?"

Her laughter was not derisive, only amused, but in a tone that went right to Munro's groin. "Does he know you and I played a little grab and kiss? No. But he did want to know why I changed my mind about living in The Hague. I told him I was tempted by a handsome, sexy Secret Service agent and decided I better come home. How is your daughter?"

Munro was concentrating on the fact that she had referred to him as handsome and sexy, then when he registered the question about his daughter, he beamed broadly. "Great. Took some counseling afterwards, but she was back studying in Dublin within a year. More careful now, though." Mai Fisher had rescued his daughter from IRA kidnappers in Ireland, and Munro had been more than grateful. Lustful.

"Good for her. I hear you're retiring."

"End of February."

"Want a job?"

"What? Where? With you?" His expression moved so fluidly from shock to enthusiasm to panic to hope that Mai had to laugh again.

"And be tempted everyday?" she teased. "No, I meant with a private security business that I have. Or were you going to leave all this excitement behind?"

"I don't know yet what I'm going to do."

"Why are you leaving then?"

Shrugging, Munro sighed. "It's time. When I start thinking of my agents as my children, I'm getting too old for this."

"I'll send you some information about my company. Have a look and then contact me with any questions you might have. Now that we've done the small talk thing, let's get back to this threatening letter from Hopewell Reborn. I've not kept up with America's fringe right wing for a while, but I can contact some analysts in my organization and get some up-to-date intelligence."

Her abrupt dismissal of their byplay hurt a bit, but he resumed his business-like demeanor. "We've verified the existence of a group that calls itself Hopewell Reborn."

"Oh, don't tell me, your Fibbie brothers have assured you of this, right?" Munro twitched a bit uncomfortably. "Well, yes. Project Meggido…"

"Plagiarized from a report I prepared back in early 1995. I suppose I could sue, but there's that plausible deniability thing. Just allow me the comfort level of having this independently verified. Am I going to be able to see that letter?"

"Yeah. It's in an evidence locker, but I can have it here in 15 minutes."

"Good. I'm assuming you're secure here, my intrusion notwithstanding?"

"Yes."

"I'll call my organization and get them working on the verification. When is your next sitrep?"

"Just under two hours."

"Let's get moving."

*   *   *

On her own secure, satellite cell phone Mai Fisher placed a call to a private number in The Hague. A sleepy voice answered, and she smiled, imagining his unclad form in bed.

"I understand your wife was away, so I thought I'd call," she said.

"She's away, but she has spies everywhere," replied her husband, Alexei Bukharin.

"She doesn't have spies. She is a spy."

"And she knows my every move. Were the Feds happy to see you?"

"So far only one, a favorable one at that, has seen me. I've faxed you a letter from a woman who calls herself Sarai. She claims to be the leader of a group called Hopewell Reborn."

"Shit," Alexei muttered. "Hang on. Let me go to the office. I'm putting you on hold."

In a few moments she heard him pick up the phone. "Yeah. I got the fax," he said.

"Anything familiar?"

"Yes. The name Sarai. She was one of Elijah's harem. I never spoke with her, but Karen told me which ones were his regulars. I think she had a child of his. The letter is pretty standard Hopewell stuff. Our analysts verified this?"

"Yes."

"Any sightings locally?"

"The analysts are going through routine surveillance photos from the area, but that takes time."

"I can't judge the level of her commitment because I never met her. I do remember Karen saying that Elijah's women were some of the most zealous adherents of Hopewell's philosophy."

"Would she be a shooter?"

"The women did get rudimentary firearms training, mostly defensive, though. Any projections on how many interracial couples could possibly show up at this thing?"

"Almost impossible to predict. Given the diversity and general attitude of tolerance in the area, there are a lot of interracial couples."

"True, but she'll be interested only in black and white couples."

"Still could be hundreds of couples, Alexei. Is it possible there could be a hit squad? Or just the one person?"

"It could be either. I don't know. I haven't been keeping up with developments with the remnants of Hopewell. Do you have an ID on this woman other than Sarai?"

"Not yet. The analysts are working on it. If she hasn't committed any crimes, any other ID will be difficult to get in such a short time."

"You get the Biblical reference?"

"Sarai was the wife of Abraham who gave her handmaiden to him when Sarai herself couldn't bear children. She later became pregnant and had the handmaiden and her child exiled. Do you think that's symbolic?"

"I don't know…" His voice trailed off.

"What?" she prompted.

"I'm trying to remember something Karen told me about a woman Elijah kicked out of Hopewell."

Mai gritted her teeth at the third utterance of the name "Karen," an undercover ATF agent in Hopewell with whom Alexei had a brief affair while he was undercover himself. Typical man, she thought to herself. He thinks because it was five years ago and she's dead that it doesn't hurt anymore. Mai waited patiently, deciding that one more mention of Karen's name, and she would comment on it.

"Yes. A woman who had one of Elijah's oldest children had a girl, then this woman who calls herself Sarai had a boy. She managed to get the other woman out of favor, and she left Hopewell. I believe she settled in Oklahoma somewhere near Hopewell because Elijah got a sympathetic judge to make sure he shared custody."

"She would be able to give us a name. A good lead. Thanks."

"I haven't given you much to go on."

"It's a start. The analysts will do what they can. Sorry I woke you."

"That's all right. It's good to hear your voice." He paused. "Why did you just fax me this today?"

"Because I just got it today."

"The Feds sat on this for two days before telling you?"

"No. I made a side trip before I came here." His silence was long and profound. "I would have told you when I got back," she added, hoping to fend off a long-distance argument.

"Why do you let him pull your chain? He whimpers about the injustice of it all, and you respond. He is where he belongs, and he will get the justice he deserves. When will you see it's because he's a coward that he keeps putting you on the guilt trip? He's not in prison because of what you failed to do but because of what he did."

"All right, well, it was wonderful talking to you as well," Mai said. "I'll check back with you if the lead you gave me produces anything."

"Go ahead, cut me off."

"I'm burning up satellite time, and I didn't call you to be reminded over and over again about your lover Karen or about my part in putting the wrong man in prison."

"Karen was not a lover."

"What else do you call someone you sleep with? This conversation is over, Alexei. I'll talk to you later."

Mai ended the call then turned off the satellite cell phone. A headache pounded behind her eyes, fueled by jet lag, frustration, and anger, anger with Alexei, with herself. He was the second man important to her that she'd displeased in the past two days.

*   *   *

Two Days Earlier
Terre Haute, Indiana

His jailhouse pallor was unchanged from her visits to him in Colorado, but his face was fleshier, his frame more filled out, the result of lack of exercise and starchy prison food. The routine was similar to what he had experienced at SuperMax in Colorado—23 hours in a 6' by 12' cell, one hour a day for "recreation" in another room with a half dozen armed guards. At SuperMax he had been allowed to converse with only two other inmates, both convicted bombers as well. He was a walking dead man, anyway, so what did it matter? He had been transferred to Indiana after the Supreme Court rejected his first appeal only because SuperMax didn't do executions.

He had always been too thin as long as she'd known him, which was only a half dozen years, most of them while he was in prison. Now some maturity and the extra weight gave him presence and confidence. He was a man in his early 30's now—and not likely to see 40—a stage where adulthood showed in the face and body language.

The guards brought him to the interview room shackled hand and foot and wearing a stun belt. One guard, who would remain in the room, would hold the control. Mai had observed all this by CCT as she stood with the warden and complained about the belt.

"Standard procedure for dangerous inmates," was the reply.

"You know his record. He's made no trouble from the time he was taken into custody, and he's certainly no threat to me," Mai countered. "Take it off him, or I'll make certain the UN Human Rights Council inspects this prison from ceiling to basement and releases its findings in an open session of the Security Council."

The belt had been removed but not the shackles, and the guard got to stand outside the door rather than inside.

When she entered and he saw her, the inmate was glad to see her, but he tried to show her indifference when she sat in a chair that was outside of his reach.

"You've put on some weight," she smiled at him.

"Yeah," he smirked. "Maybe I'll get so fat that the dosage won't be enough, huh?"

Gallows humor, or more appropriately, lethal injection humor.

"How is your family?" she asked, ignoring it.

"The same," he answered, shrugging. "My mother says it upsets her too much to see me here, so she doesn't want to come."

"I'm sure it does upset her."

"It's just her excuse. My dad is glad I'm closer, but he doesn't drive long trips anymore, and my sister." Another shrug. "Is too busy getting on with her life. And you haven't come in a year."

"We talked about that. If I come, it takes a visitor period away from your family."

"Another excuse. What's the real reason you haven't been here?"

"I have a job, one where it's not so easy to get away from."

"Out spying on more people?"

"I've been in the Balkans, mostly," she said, conceding him some information. Who would he tell, and who would believe him? If his story were checked, it would meet a dead end. It perked his interest, though.

"Where?"

"Kosovo."

"Were you there during the bombing?"

"Before and after."

"See any action?"

"A little. Mostly I saw man's inhumanity to man, and woman, and children."

"So, you supported the bombing?"

"I had a simpler solution, but one that wasn't really viable."

"What was it?"

"A 'private' conference with Slobodan Milosevic."

He laughed at that. "Somehow I think old Slobo wouldn't like the outcome of that meeting too much."

"Now, you can be honest with me. How are you really doing?"

His hardness softened even more. "When they transferred me here, it became real, you know. The only reason I'm here is that they don't kill people in SuperMax. As long as I was in Colorado I could pretend I was like the Unabomber, you know. A lifer." His winning smile appeared. "Actually, I am a lifer. Just a short-timer."

"Don't give me the bullshit you gave the press about knowing when you were going to die being a blessing."

"Yeah, well. They expect the heartless bomber to make a joke of life, don't they?"

"Why give them what they expect?"

"Because I don't give a fuck anymore. Nobody gives a fuck about me. Why should I care?"

"I care."

"Right. I don't see you for a year. I leave phone messages, and it takes you days or weeks to call back."

"Don't."

"Look, I just want this to be over with."

"Then, tell your lawyers no more appeals."

"I can't. I can't let my family think I've given in. Sometimes I wish I'd have a stroke or a heart attack, but, hell, they give me physicals to make sure I'm in good health when they kill me. I wouldn't even be able to try to kill myself, being under 24-hour watch. If you care, you'd put me out of my fucking misery."

"I couldn't do that before. What makes you think I could do it now?"

"You killed that FBI agent in cold blood. Why not me?"

"He deserved it."

"And I'm the Oklahoma City Bomber, the Monster, Evil Incarnate. Don't I deserve it?"

"Some people think so, but I don't. You were misled by a monster who was evil incarnate."

"Sounds like typical liberal excuse-making."

"Look, if you think I'm going to increase the number of my visits to listen to you feel sorry for yourself, you're asking a lot."

She saw his resolve fade, replaced by his easily manifest vulnerability. "I'm sorry, Maggie," he said, using the only name he knew her by. "I just get down sometimes."

"I wonder why?" she mused.

He blinked his eyes several times, spots of red flaring on his cheeks, the only evidence of his feeling emotion. "You remember that morning in the motel in Kingman where I took you after Elijah beat you?"

How could she forget. She had her gun pressed against his chest, and she hadn't been able to pull the trigger. If she had, neither of them would be here right now, and 169 people would be alive.

"Yes."

"Sometimes I have this dream where we're there, and you do pull the trigger."

She closed her eyes in pain. "I have the same dream," she whispered.

"You could do it," he whispered back. "You could find a way. Make it look like heart failure or something. You could do that."

"Don't ask me for that. Ask for me something I can give you."

"What I want is to be free, and the only way I'm going to be free is to die."

She had once told the people who would prosecute the man before her that the worst punishment they could give him was to take away his liberty, that killing him would be a release. He was proving her prophetic.

"I told you before. Another wrong won't make a right," she said. "Enough people have died over this."

"And I'll be the last, but what will I be in three years, five years when they finally kill me? Mad? I can feel my mind slipping away from me. They won't let me have my music. They won't let me read what I want to read. They censor the news I get. I'm just becoming lost."

"You were lost before," she said, "when you listened to Elijah."

"Elijah gave me purpose."

"He sold you a bill of goods. He was too much of a coward to do the job himself, so he conned you into it. And don't fool yourself into thinking he'll keep any of the so-called promises he made to you."

"Maybe he'll end up being the only person I can rely on," he challenged her.

Mai shook her head ruefully. "You don't even get it. He put you here. Now you have to live with it. Or die with it, as the case may be."

"Prophet won't tell anybody when he moves."

"Prophet is dead," Mai said. "He died from the bomb he made you drive up to a building full of people."

"He's in hiding…"

"No. He was there, and he died there. That mysterious extra leg your first lawyer tried to focus the jury on? That was all that was left of Elijah."

He turned her logic on her. "So, you're all I have left. Are you going to let me down, too?"

"That's the problem, isn't it? Everyone let you down. The Army, the government, your mother, Prophet, me. Did you ever stop to think how many people you let down when you parked that truck in front of the

Murrah building then ran away? Jesus, take some responsibility for your actions at least once before you die."

The spots of color deepened on his cheeks, and his eyes became flat and emotionless, the face he showed the world and which led to the myth that he was an unfeeling monster.

"You can leave now with a clear conscience," he said, his voice choked with the feelings he tried to hide. "You don't have to come back."

"You can't deny that fundamental thing, that basic act. I was there, remember? You want to die easy, then live up to what you did."

"I will when you will."

"I have."

"Really?" he said, sardonically. "I don't see you sitting here waiting for your government to shove a needle in your veins." He stood up and walked over the door, meeting the guard eye to eye as he looked into the room. "I'm ready to go back," he said.

"Step back from the door," the guard ordered, and the condemned murderer of 168 people obeyed without question.

Mai softly called his name.

"No," he tossed over his shoulder. "If you're going to let me down, just leave me alone."

"I'll keep my promise to you," she said as the guard took him into custody. The promise to be beside him when he died. The look he gave as he was led away in shackles was angry, but she saw the relief.

*   *   *

December 30, 1999

Twelve hours after she arrived in Washington, DC, Mai Fisher found herself back on her private airplane headed for the state of Oklahoma, a trip she had hoped never to make again. William Henry Munro accompanied her this time, in spite of her protests that he was needed at his command post. His second was capable, he countered, and it was incumbent upon him to follow up this lead. After all, she wasn't on an official UN mission. If the woman the UN analysts had located needed to be taken into custody, it would have to be done so under his law enforcement authority.

A check of court records in Lawton, Oklahoma revealed that there was a custody order allowing "Elijah Hopewell" visitation rights with his daughter at her mother's home, a home which Hopewell's funds had provided for her, free and clear of liens and mortgages. The records also conveniently provided the address, where Mai and Munro headed in a rental car after landing at the local small airport at Lawton. Just in case it was needed, Munro brought along a warrant issued quickly by a federal judge in Washington.

The ranch-style house was common in Oklahoma, its size and shape not much different from the abode it was a step up from—a double-wide trailer. It was well-kept and surrounded by a six foot-high, chain link fence festooned with "No Trespassing" and "Beware of Dog" signs. When the two stepped from the car and approached the gate, they saw the reason for the latter sign. From around behind the house charged a beefy Rottweiler, teeth barred, a growl ululating from its throat. The dog launched himself at the fence, making Munro take an involuntary step back, but stopped just short of crashing into it. Mai stood her ground.

"Easy, boy," she tried. The dog began a fierce barking, snapping at them from behind the fence. "Well, it was worth a try," she muttered.

The door to the house opened, and the muzzle of a shotgun emerged. Munro's hand snaked under his coat, but Mai put a hand on his arm.

"Ms. Harper," Mai called out, dropping most of the English accent from her voice. "Could you call off the dog so that we can talk?"

The shotgun's muzzle swung slowly toward them, and Mai felt Munro's arm tense again. "Easy, Munro," she said. "A scatter gun can't do us much harm from there."

Munro snorted and called out, "Federal Agent, Ms. Harper. I have a warrant."

"Oh, that's going to make an impression on a Hopewell follower, Munro," Mai said under her breath.

The door opened wider, and a woman in her late 30's appeared, cradling the shotgun on her arm. Her laughter reached them.

"Well, that's going to make me piss my pants," she told them. "Can't you Feds read? No trespassing."

"We need to ask you some questions," Munro tried again.

"Ask them," Carlene Harper said.

"Could we come in?"

"I'm not about to get Weavered," Harper answered. "Ask them from there or leave."

Munro held up the warrant. "I have a warrant," he repeated.

"Munro…" Mai muttered at him.

Harper's laughter reached them again. "Ya'll better get back in your car and get the hell out of here. If I shoot you and drag you inside the gate, who do you think the local law will believe? The Federal Government," she said in a sneer, "or a helpless woman living alone trying to protect herself?"

"If we leave, more of us will come back," Munro threatened.

"And I'll be gone before you and your jackboots can get here."

Mai turned to Munro. "May I try?" Without waiting for his answer, Mai took a step or two closer to the fence, ignoring the growls of the dog. "Ms. Harper, do you remember Sarai?"

"How do you know about Sarai?"

"I know she had you kicked out of Hopewell, you and your daughter, Elijah's first born."

"What about her?"

"I need to know her real name."

"Why?"

"To stop her from something she's planning."

"Against ZOG?"

"No, against innocent people. She says she's doing it in Prophet's name, but does she have the right to that?"

"No. I was the first. She cast me out."

"That's right. She did. Do you want her to be remembered as the one who carried on Prophet's legacy?"

The silence extended, but Mai watched the consideration on the woman's face. Finally, an expression of determination overcame the distrust. Mai felt her own heart race at the prospect of what the woman was about to say.

"Amelia Saint Claire," Carlene Harper said. "Now, get away from here or I open the gate electronically and let Adolph at you."

She went back inside and closed the door.

"Adolph?" Mai said. "These people are not very original. Let's go, Munro, before she lets loose the dog of war."

Munro stood there for a moment wondering why he was surprised then joined her in the car.

"How do you know," he asked when they were a mile or two away, "that she isn't calling Sarai right now and warning her?"

"Because she hates her more than she hates ZOG," Mai replied.

"How do you know…"

"I spent the good part of two years immersed in their crap. I know." She pulled her satellite cell phone out of a pocket and handed it to him. "Let's not waste any time. Amelia Saint Claire wasn't always Sarai. Get your people started tracking her down."

*   *   *

That evening when Munro walked with Mai Fisher back into the Command Center, he was met by his second in command, a no-nonsense FBI agent in her mid-40's.

"Report," Munro said.

"Vitals search showed us 153 Amelia Saint Claire's. Only one in Idaho. At least that's where she was up until six months ago," the agent reported.

"What happened six months ago?" Mai asked.

The woman looked at Munro, who nodded, then turned back to Mai. "She applied for unemployment benefits from a truck stop waitress job. She collected benefits for about eight weeks. Then nothing. We have a picture from Idaho. She did have a driver's license." She handed over an eight by 10 blow up of a typical driver's license photograph. The woman in the picture was the poster girl for sullen. Mousy blonde hair was pulled up into a knot on the top of her head, and she was without makeup. Hers was a nondescript face, one that you could lose easily in a crowd, and Mai sought in vain for some distinguishing characteristic.

"She generally matches the description of a woman who has held up three banks, a gun shop, and a pawn shop," continued the FBI agent.

"How much money from the robberies?" Mai asked. Again, the agent waited for a nod from Munro.

"$10,000 from one, $7,500 and $5,000 from the other two."

"What was taken from the gun store and pawn shop?"

"Shotguns, .45 caliber handguns, an Uzi." Mai canted an eyebrow at the latter gun. "In the gun store owner's, ah, private collection."

"So, she's armed herself and financed herself. Where's her child?" Mai asked.

"With relatives in Idaho," responded the FBI agent. "They live inside Aryan Nations."

Mai was still staring at the photo. "Where was the pawn shop robbery and how long ago?" she asked.

"In Pittsburgh, Pennsylvania three weeks ago."

"Do you have any surveillance on William Pierce's place in West Virginia?" Mai asked.

"National Alliance?" the FBI agent queried, and Mai nodded. "Only occasionally. Why?"

"Sometimes when these lone wolves go underground, they go from compound to compound or safe house to safe house where they know they'll be welcomed," Mai replied. "Where no one will ask questions. But if Ms. Saint Claire has been living in Aryan Nations she's been getting a good dose of the Louis Beam philosophy of leaderless resistance. It will do no good to question anyone in AN or at the National Alliance. It's doubtful they'd acknowledge that she was there, and even if she were, they wouldn't know what she was up to."

"So, what do we do?" asked the FBI agent.

"Short of calling off the whole thing tomorrow night, keep your eyes open," came a man's voice from the direction of Munro's office.

Mai and Munro turned to look, and the FBI agent said, "Agent Munro, I didn't get a chance to tell you. This gentleman arrived this morning from the UN Secretary-General's office."

The three of them looked on a man in his mid to late 50's, white hair, high cheekbones, broad forehead, blue eyes surrounded by blond, nearly white eyelashes, a small scar bisecting his right eyebrow. He was a couple of inches taller than six feet, broad-shouldered, and dressed to the nines in an expensive double-breasted, black suit beneath which he wore a charcoal turtleneck. Brushing below the suit's collar, his hair was thick, full, and combed back off his face from a widow's peak. The smile he wore was sardonic, but it only served his romance novel looks and had the desired effect on the butchy FBI agent. She blushed slightly.

"Agent Munro," Mai began, "I don't believe you've had the pleasure of meeting my husband, Alexei Bukharin."

The FBI agent's disappointment when she heard the word "husband" was as acute as Munro's discomfort, and Mai noted Alexei seemed to enjoy both.

"Alexei," Mai continued, "this is Special Agent William Munro of the Secret Service."

Alexei walked forward and extended his hand to Munro for a shake, and Munro squared his shoulders before he and Alexei shook hands.

Mai watched the handshake go on a bit long and saw that the knuckles of each man's right hand went white. Wonderful, she thought.

Alexei released Munro's hand. "Pleased to meet you, Agent Munro. I've heard quite a few compliments about your work."

Munro glanced at Mai then back to Alexei. "And I've heard a lot about you, Agent Bukharin," he said.

"No longer Agent Bukharin," Alexei said with a smile. "Special Representative Bukharin now, but, please, call me Alexei. I'm only here in a semi-official capacity."

"Semi-official?" Munro queried.

"My wife faxed me a copy of the threatening letter you received. I was inside Hopewell, and I thought it best that I at least be on hand as a resource."

Mai handed over the photo. "This is Amelia Saint Claire, aka Sarai."

Alexei took the picture and brought out reading glasses from his inside jacket pocket. They were half glasses that he perched on the bridge of his aquiline nose as he studied the photo.

"She was a few years younger, of course, and I only encountered her at meetings, but that's she," he replied.

"You obviously overheard the information we were just provided," Mai said.

"About the robberies, yes," he said, smiling, though he had noticed the tightness in her tone. He looked back to Munro. "How many officers will you have in and around the crowd?"

Munro looked to his second. "Brenda, what was the last count?"

"As of noon tomorrow, we'll have 7,439 police and other law enforcement agents on duty at the Main Street Millennium and at the Mall," Brenda responded.

"You need to get the copy machines going," Alexei said. "Every officer needs a copy of that picture. Tell them she should be considered armed and extremely dangerous. She's been indoctrinated that any law enforcement officer is an agent of a godless government out to kill her.

She'll act to protect herself if she suspects any police officer has an interest in her. Don't let them be fooled by her diminutive size. She thinks she's on a mission from Yahweh. You've got surveillance cameras throughout the Mall?"

Munro and his second shifted a bit uncomfortably.

"Your secret is safe with me," Alexei assured. "I'll want to be somewhere where I can observe the monitors. I might be able to spot her. I'll need to be linked in so that I can direct officers to her if I do." Munro and Brenda didn't indicate assent. "Is there some problem here?"

"Agent Munro isn't quite accustomed to your take-charge demeanor, Alexei. Besides, you know how Feds can be when we show up," Mai said.

"Agent Munro," Alexei soothed, "I'm not here to usurp anyone's authority. I'm a resource, and a good one, as my partner can attest to. That's all I'm proposing to be to you. If you object to my being linked into your communications, then I don't have to be, but it would help things. Any movement of agents, any proposed action would be your call."

"Pardon my reticence, Mr. Bukharin," Munro said, "but I wasn't exactly expecting you to show up."

"Munro," Mai said, "can I speak with you privately?"

"What?"

"Outside a moment, please," she said and walked outside the Command Center.

"Excuse me," Munro said and followed.

Outside, Mai turned on him, up in his face. "Munro, do not treat Alexei as if he's washed up or as if he's some sort of rival to you. He's neither."

"I don't know what you mean."

"Please. The two of you nearly arm-wrestled, and the very air is testosterone-laden. Alexei can help you, so let him do what he can do best. This attitude is what fucked things up at Waco and Oklahoma City, and if it doesn't change, both of us will go back to The Hague and leave you to find the needle in this particular haystack."

"Is that why he's here?"

"Partly."

"What's the other part?"

"That I'm here with you."

"I thought you said he didn't know what happened."

"Once again, Munro, you're surprised that I can lie with impunity. Of course he knows because I told him. That's what married people do. We discussed it, and he accepted the circumstances under which our kissing occurred. He and I are in a continual state of working on our marriage, and we agreed long ago that honesty needed to be a part of it. He holds nothing against you, so give him the benefit of the doubt and use his talents where they can be of benefit."

"Well, hell, Mai, if we're going to do honesty, then understand this. I like you. I really do, and not just because you helped, no, you saved my daughter. And yes, I was hoping we could work together on this, just us, like we did before because you are just about the most attractive damn thing that has come along in my life in many a year. And I am a man, after all."

Mai grinned. "You're jealous of my husband? This is quite the turn. It's supposed to be the other way around."

"No shit, Sherlock. I'm just a dumb Fed. What do you expect?"

"Well, I'm flattered. Now, can we go do some work?"

"Hell, what do you think?"

Back inside, Alexei had said something that left Brenda the FBI agent giggling girlishly. She again blushed slightly when Munro and Mai entered and murmured something about making a perimeter check before exiting the Command Center. Mai shook her head at him, but Alexei maintained a look of utter innocence.

"So, are we working together?" he asked Munro.

"Of course, Mr. Bukharin," Munro said. "Come into my office, both of you, and let's work out a plan." Munro disappeared into the innards of the Command Center.

"Now, why do you suppose he won't call me Alexei?" Alexei asked Mai.

"Could it be because you're being a prick toward him?"

"Maybe. You were upset when we spoke yesterday."

"Is that why you came?"

"Mainly. I'm sorry I so casually mentioned Karen. I consider it behind me, but that doesn't mean I should assume it's behind us."

"You know, you have this uncanny knack for knowing when I'm absolutely pissed at you and apologizing before I ever get to make my points."

"Well-developed over the years of being married. I've come to read you pretty well. Would you like for me to apologize to Agent Munro as well?"

"I'll leave that entirely up to you." She stepped up to him, leaned up on her toes, and kissed his lips lightly. "I'm glad you're here."

"I'm really jet-lagged, but I think if you took me home, I could make you even gladder."

"Later. After we plan." She nodded toward Munro's office then headed there.

"Obviously, we have some work to do on priorities," Alexei murmured, then followed.

*   *   *

December 31, 1999

Beneath her breath she prayed, pleas to her Creator to shield her from the godlessness surrounding her. Young women displaying themselves, men looking at them with depravity. Any of them could be agents of ZOG, so she needed that shield that only her Lord could provide. Yet whenever a young family passed by her with children, she ached for her son with a palpable pain. She did this for her son, to make a proper world for her child to grow up in. It was what the child's father had died for. It was what he said to her in her dreams every night.

She was quite clear on and committed to what she had to do for Elijah, and through him, for Yahweh, but her only regret was never seeing her child again. That she had left him with Yahweh-fearing people who would raise him to be proud of his race and to plant his seed for that race was some solace, but Amelia Saint Claire would have liked to have held her fine, Aryan grandsons in her arms. Elijah's voice, to her the voice of Yahweh himself, spoke and assured her that she would be able to see her child and her future grandchildren from his side in heaven.

That she would go to Paradise and be with Elijah and Yashua and Yahweh, she had no doubt. She had been a faithful servant of Yahweh, bearing Elijah's child, enduring the breakup of Hopewell, the uncertain future, and Elijah's death. There had never been a body, but she knew. He would have returned to her, his true wife, had he been able. Then, the visitations had started, first his beautiful, soothing, inspiring voice, then his form itself, gossamer, like an angel, shining his light on her.

At first she had resisted what he told her she needed to do. After all, bloodletting was the holy cause and work of Aryan Warriors. An Aryan woman's duty was to accept the Warriors' seed, bear the next generation of warriors, and teach the daughters their duty. But her heavenly husband, Elijah the Prophet, had been persuasive, and Amelia, always called Sarai by her beloved, had prevailed upon the men at Aryan Nations to teach her. An apt pupil, she had earned their praise and continued instruction when she was free with her affections. Elijah had forgiven her, explaining that she had to do whatever was necessary to carry out his bidding. She had trained well, improving her accuracy and speed with multiple weapons. She waited and practiced until Elijah chose to impart to her the time and event, and when he had explained it, Sarai marveled at his timing. In death he was what he had been in life, symbolic. What better occasion to herald the End Times than the false millennium? A war between the races will bring on the End Times, Elijah taught. So, she, a proud white woman, would walk among the godless, be tainted by their filth, and bring Elijah's wrath down on the race-mixers, the miscegenous. They and their mongrel pups would die.

At times the crowds and their ebullience threatened to overwhelm her, and she longed for the quiet beauty of the Idaho mountains and the long walks she would take with her son at her side, telling him of his father in heaven and the destiny that awaited him. How she would miss that, and she had to force herself not to dwell on what could have been. Focus, came Elijah's voice. Focus and open herself to the possibilities.

There. Just yards away. Her stomach churned with nausea, and her mouth turned down in a scowl. A nigger with a beautiful, blonde Aryan woman on his arm. Sarai wanted to weep and beat her breast. How could she? How could this flower of Aryan womanhood debase herself? No, Elijah warned, she couldn't think of the whore as an Aryan woman anymore. Once you lie down with filth, you become filth. There was no child with them, but perhaps, came the thought, the whore carried a mongrel monster inside her defiled womb. Sarai would weep later for the lost womb that would not bear Aryan warriors, but now she had to give herself over to her holy cause.

As the unknowing young couple pressed through the crowd, laughing and looking forward to the entertainment that represented America, Sarai touched the warmth of her sawed off shotgun hidden beneath her over-large raincoat and followed them, murmuring prayers she knew Elijah heard.

*   *   *

The evening was unseasonably warm for the end of December, and that made people more enthusiastic. For the most part, there was little booze to intensify the celebratory attitude of the crowds, and there was general politeness. A true family affair, adults strolled arm in arm and surrounded by their broods of all ages. The backdrop of Washington, DC's monuments made the scene quintessentially American. The entertainment portion at the Lincoln Memorial had already started, but Mai found she could pay little attention to it on any of the various huge screens placed for those who couldn't get close enough to the makeshift stage on the Memorial's steps.

There was an air of excitement but no boisterousness, merely good-natured cheering and applause for the varied musical acts. A part of Mai wished she could join them rather than walk among them looking for the dark side of American society, trying to tune out the revelry while she listened to a constant stream of conversation on the command frequency in her left ear. In her right ear was an occasional comment from Alexei on their own discreet frequency. A bit of a subterfuge, but Alexei felt more comfortable being able to access her without anyone knowing about it. And, even after all this time and including nearly two years working on her own, Mai was comforted and reassured by his voice. It reminded her of their early days together when he was still her training agent. His voice, always calm and steady, could encourage her to do things she never thought she was capable of. He could also admonish, but he had rarely lost his temper with her—professionally. Their personal life during that same time was hardly that collegial, but they had survived both the professional and the personal dangers. They were together, and that was all that mattered. Mai glanced around at the many older couples sharing the evening and wished that she and Alexei could be one of them.

No, she thought, their personal happiness was not all that mattered, and a normal life was not theirs to embrace nor could it ever be. Normal for them was a world where the search for truth and the obtaining of justice from that truth was all-important, and no desk job could change that. Alexei had made that point to her 20 years ago, and her denial then echoed his now.

Such thoughts were a distraction, and she pushed them away. Their relationship had been ever-evolving, and they led a different life now, did a new kind of work. The fulfillment in that work was elusive, but she would find it.

She had to.

*   *   *

Alexei rubbed first one eye then the other so he could keep at least one trained on the images transmitted from the numerous security cameras around the Mall. Munro paced behind him, his voice a murmur as he kept up a continual conversation over the radio. Munro was sweating. Alexei was cool. Munro was tense. Alexei relaxed. Munro was a divorced, repressed Catholic, and last night and this morning Alexei had demonstrated to Mai that he was anything but. He knew Mai had seen through his performance, but she had enjoyed it anyway. He really didn't see Munro as a rival, but Munro was another of Mai's inadvertent conquests. Some men wanted to be her willing slaves on sight, while others took a while to get to that stage. The remainder couldn't stand her but wanted to fuck her anyway. With a smile, he wondered which group he fell into and decided it was an exclusive group of one who loved and respected her more than his own life.

Alexei had been scanning video screens for hours, knowing that spotting Amelia Saint Claire, aka Sarai, was unlikely at best. The only hope was that with the obviously increased security, she would back down from the threat in her letter to "erase the scourge of miscegenation" from the "capital of Yahweh's greatest nation." Alexei surmised that was what Munro was telling himself to stay optimistic in the face of a nearly impossible task. Munro could afford that optimism; he hadn't lived within Hopewell and been subjected to the constant racism, nationalism, neo-Nazism, and Christian Identity. At the end of his undercover mission there, Alexei found himself so steeped in the propaganda that he had trouble re-associating in his usual life. Of course, his infidelity while there had been no help to his reentry. Though he had never personally met Amelia Saint Claire, being involved now in her crusade forced him to remember things about Hopewell he had wanted to forget.

Elijah's daily racist vitriol he called sermons.

Alexei's own role, while undercover, in teaching people to kill.

Pretending to believe in the garbage spewed out in Hopewell's publications and videos.

Finding solace in an incredibly brave woman, a Jewish ATF agent who had been undercover in Hopewell two years longer than he.

For her to have survived Hopewell and the bounty placed on the two of them by Elijah after their escape then to die as a victim of a coward's bomb was something that still made him angry, an anger he couldn't shed because he wasn't able to discuss his feelings with Mai. She would interpret his anger over Karen's death as a sign he cared for her. And of course he had, just not in the way he cared for Mai. Karen had been convenient, much as Mai had been in their early years together, and Alexei had used Karen to keep his sanity while in Hopewell. As a result, he had disappointed everyone.

Alexei, he told himself, you are getting old, dwelling on depressing events from the past. That past is past, and the future… Suddenly, he couldn't fill in the blank of a future which seemed so certain to him a few days ago.

Before he could wallow in the implications of that, a figure on one of the screens caught his eye, and he felt a familiar surge of adrenaline. Without betraying himself to Munro, Alexei typed in a command on the keyboard that would localize that camera. Then, he switched to a joystick to zoom in. The picture was grainy and indistinct, and Alexei held the only photo they had of Sarai next to the video screen. The image from the video camera wasn't exactly face on, but about three-quarters. The nose was the same. The ear pattern, nearly as distinctive as fingerprints, was the same. Unobtrusively, he switched off the transmitter that Munro was on and switched over to the UN frequency.

"Mai, where are you?" he murmured.

A few seconds went by as she made the switch herself. "I'm about midway on the south side of the Reflecting Pool," she replied. "What is it?"

"I have her." He backed the camera off, watched as Sarai left the frame and was picked up by the next camera. Alexei took control of that camera and focused it on Sarai then noted the location. "She's directly opposite you and slightly ahead. She's following an interracial couple. She's wearing a denim duster, unbuttoned."

"Uzi or sawed-off shotgun?"

"I won't speculate except to say expect both."

"All right, I'm moving toward that sector. I'm presuming you want me to handle this on my own?"

"Do you want help?"

"Not right now, but you'll be the first to know."

"I'm tracking you, and I reserve the right to send the cavalry on my call."

"I've always trusted your judgement. You won't hear from me again until I spot her, but keep on updating."

Alexei acknowledged then debated with himself briefly. Quickly, he made his decision. "Munro," he called out.

"Yeah?" Munro came and stood at his shoulder, saw that Alexei had isolated someone on one of the video feeds. "You found her?"

"I'm pretty sure. Mai is on her way to intercept."

"Only Mai?"

Alexei turned and looked up at the man. "She's in a very crowded area. Potential for a lot of collateral damage."

Munro's jaw clenched. "The Secret Service is not the FBI," he said. "Our cowboy quotient is low."

Alexei grinned. "'Cowboy quotient?' An apt description. Can you alert only your agents?"

"You're not the only one around her with a discreet transmitter and frequency. Give me the particulars."

The information was passed along, and a quick plan worked out. Mai was advised and almost immediately responded, "I have her."

"Confirm identity," Alexei said.

"Confirmed. I'm going past her then coming up behind."

"I have you on camera," Alexei said. He murmured something to her in Russian, and with her lyrical laugh, she responded in kind.

"What did you say?" Munro asked.

"Hmm, what?" Alexei said distractedly.

"I thought that was only her annoying habit, speaking in foreign languages."

Alexei turned in his chair and looked up at Munro. "It was nothing tactical," he said. "I simply told her I loved her. A superstition of mine. She finds it amusing."

Munro shook his head. "The two of you have to be the strangest married couple I've ever known."

"Were you hoping it was a marriage of convenience?"

"Frankly, yes. Not just because she saved my daughter, but she's just one hell of a woman."

"Of that I'm well aware. Sorry to disappoint you. We are quite fond of each other. We have our ups and downs. Right now is an up. When she helped you out, we were in a down, but I am grateful for whatever liberties you took."

"What?"

"It sent her running back to me. So, thank you."

"Not exactly Good Housingkeeping ideal, but you're welcome, I guess."

*   *   *

Mai quickly slipped by Sarai, who was so focused on her quarry she had pushed everything else aside. Mai turned abruptly and came up behind her, within an arm's length. The over-sized coat Sarai wore hid whatever weapons she had, and Mai didn't like the fact she couldn't assess what she was up against. The entertainment was rapidly approaching its conclusion, and Mai stole a glance at her watch. Seven minutes before midnight.

Softly, so close was she to Sarai, Mai transmitted, "Sitrep."

"Four agents, approximately eight minutes away," Alexei responded.

Not enough time. Sarai was going to do whatever she had in mind no doubt on the stroke of midnight.

"You're incredibly close," Alexei said. "Back off until the others arrive." When she didn't move he said, "Mai?"

Mai knew he could still see her, so she had no qualms in switching off her radio. As comforting as his voice had been, now it would only distract her. She reached inside her own coat, brought out the Beretta, hiding it with her body, and let the crowd do its work. When she was jostled into Sarai's back, Mai got a grip on the woman's coat and pushed the muzzle of the Beretta into her side.

Mai whispered into Sarai's ear, "Move and you're dead right here."

"I smell ZOG on you," Sarai hissed. "You can't stop me. I have Yahweh in my heart and Elijah at my side."

"Elijah is in hell. We're going to turn to the right and walk toward the street where we'll be met by some of my fellow agents of ZOG. If I have to shoot you and drag you out of here I'll do it."

*   *   *

"What the hell is she doing now?" Munro demanded.

"Improvising," Alexei said, standing. From beneath his jacket he removed a Taurus PT 111 and chambered a round. "You have some spare body armor in my size?"

*   *   *

Mai's captive was reluctant to move, but she did, resisting as much as possible.

"You keep me from Yahweh's work," Sarai said.

"I'll let Yahweh take it up with me personally. Move faster or I'll …"

Someone had trained Sarai very well. Simultaneously, she elbowed Mai in the stomach and kicked her in the shin. Mai's body armor blunted the stomach blow, but the thick-soled boot heel against her unguarded shin brought her to the ground. Cursing, Mai rubbed the offended shin as she watched Sarai take off running, away from the crowd. Getting to her feet and following in a limping run, Mai switched her radio back on.

"She's on the move," she panted, "headed north, crossing Constitution at…" She glanced up at a street sign. "18th."

"We're converging on your position," Alexei replied. "She'll soon be out of camera range anyway."

Ignoring the stab of pain every time she landed a running step on her right foot, Mai ran, barely managing to keep Sarai in sight. The focus of the crowds was the Mall entertainment, so the people here on these streets were few, but enough to scatter when they saw the two running women, especially Mai with the Beretta in hand. Mai ran a map of DC through her head, and realized that Sarai had studied the area as well, given her confident, headlong run. Likely, she had stashed a car somewhere outside the tow-zone for the Mall events and was headed directly for it. Sarai made a sharp right turn, and breathlessly Mai gave the new position. With every step, Mai, in good shape and a daily runner, was gaining on her, but how long she could keep that up with her lower leg throbbing, she wasn't sure. Then, as if some of Mai's Irish luck decided to show up, Sarai turned into the mouth of what she obviously thought was a street, but was actually the courtyard of an office building. She was trapped. Mai kept running but brought the Beretta up, gripped in both hands. Sarai turned nearly two circles, seeking a way out, and when she saw there was none, she pulled the shotgun out from under her duster.

Mai was still far enough away that the shotgun would do little harm, unless, of course, it was loaded with slugs and not buckshot.

"No! No! No!" Mai said, authoritatively, like the glorified cop she now was. "Down! Put it down now! Drop it!"

"You drop it!" Sarai countered.

They stared each other down, both panting to catch their breath.

"There's no where to go," Mai said.

"Yahweh will show me the way," Sarai said.

"Well, he better part the Red Sea or something right about now, because you're going to have a lot of heat showing up soon."

Sarai's face split in a rapturous grin. "You can kill me, but you can't kill Elijah. He goes on. He lives. In me. In every white warrior on earth."

Something cued Mai, a tensing of Sarai's muscles or a change of facial expression, but she quickly turned and dived for the cover of a large cement planter. The shotgun blast was amplified by the enclosed courtyard, making Mai's ears ring. She rolled into a crouch behind the planter and saw that Sarai did the same behind another. Mai checked her spare magazines. In addition to the 15-round clip in the Beretta, she had two more full magazines. Without wasting shots, she could hold out until help arrived, and she quickly and quietly broadcast her position to the converging back-up teams. The shotgun sounded again, tearing up paving tiles three feet in front of the planter. Mai ventured a quick peek around the side of the planter, saw a sliver of the denim duster. Not enough to target but enough to get her attention. Mai answered with a single shot that kicked up cement shards from the planter Sarai hid behind.

"Careful," Mai said, over the radio. "There's only one way in, and she's got it in her sights."

"Do you object to being tear-gassed?" Alexei asked.

"Whatever it takes to not get anyone killed," she said.

The Secret Service didn't just tear-gas the courtyard. They lobbed in two flash-bangs before the gas, making Mai think that it was part of a plan to deafen her, but the light and noise had their effect. Amelia "Sarai" Saint Claire was stunned sufficiently that she was taken into custody without another shot being fired. When the "fireworks" ended in the courtyard, the National Mall exploded in celebration of an event that was actually a year away.

*   *   *

January 1, 2000

Mai rinsed her eyes one more time and peered at herself in the bathroom mirror. Two days with little sleep and a good dose of tear gas, and she looked as if she'd been on a week-long drunk or a three-day crying jag. How attractive. She pulled paper towels from the dispenser and dabbed her face dry. She blew her nose, which was running about as much as her eyes were, and washed her hands before leaving the bathroom in the Treasury Department. The Secret Service was using ATF facilities to interrogate Amelia Saint Claire. To the glee of the law enforcement officials, she had disavowed her need for an attorney, saying that Yahweh would guide her words. Mai had argued unsuccessfully that a lawyer should be called in anyway, and Sarai was spilling her guts. Such as they were. She spoke of Elijah as a living entity, and that had made Alexei pale. Now, as she stood in the doorway of the restroom, she saw him pacing, still pale. She stepped back inside and closed the door.

She had known exactly what tonight's outcome was going to be. Just as they had for so many years, she and Alexei had planned a mission and executed it flawlessly, the result never in doubt. God, she had missed it. When the adrenaline had pumped upon her sighting of Sarai, Mai had felt heady, almost as if she'd taken a hit of cocaine. She had taken a situation into her own hands and managed it, saved lives, made a difference. That was the point. Before, even with the perspective of what she believed were her failures, she had always made a difference. In a few days, she would be back at The Hague, making out personnel schedules, spot-checking security procedures, and filling out endless paperwork. She would never have noticed the contrast and now be depressed about it if William Henry Munro hadn't summoned her. She knew something else as well. She could not go back to The Hague.

Mai left the restroom and walked up to Alexei. He stopped pacing and faced her. She lay her palms on his chest, and he lay his hands atop hers.

"Are you all right?" she asked, a frown of concern creasing the space between her brows.

"I've been running 0902 April 19, 1995 through my head again and making sure I did see Elijah die," he replied. "The way she talks about him." He shook his head.

"She is delusional. Either that or he really is the second coming of Christ, in which case, we are all in trouble."

Alexei laughed, taking her face in his hands. "You must have driven the nuns insane," he said.

"Between my blasphemy and my, let's see, what did Sister Ignatious call it? My 'heathen, hedonistic proclivities,' yes, I pretty much kept them on their toes."

"You look as if you've been crying for a week."

"And my ears are still ringing. Do they need us any more, or can we please go home?"

"Home would be nice. I put a bottle of Dom Perignon to chill for today."

Oh God, she thought. Do I tell him or do I leave in the middle of his post-coital sleep like a coward?

"It's six a.m., Alexei," she chided.

"It is never too early for good champagne."

"I see they raised at least one hedonist in the Ukraine. I'll go tell Munro we're leaving. Where the hell did we leave the car anyway?"

"Basement of the Justice Department. I'll wait here for you, a discreet distance away in case you want to thrill Munro with a goodbye kiss."

"Tempt me, and I'll give him one that will last him all year long."

Munro was standing before the one-way window watching the "interrogation" of Amelia Saint Claire. His arms were crossed over his chest, and Mai studied his profile for a moment. It was an elegant profile, patrician where Alexei's was unaffected. Both had attractions for her, Alexei's of more depth; yet, from more than a year ago, she remembered Munro's mouth on hers, his hands fumbling to release her bra. Emotions pent up from the rescue of his kidnapped daughter, and her own lack of Alexei's physical attentions had nearly done them in. Devotion to her married state had won out, but it had been a pleasant interlude.

So, she thought, why then do you feel compelled to tell him goodbye?

*   *   *

"Munro?" he heard her call, quietly.

Munro turned to her and smiled brightly. "You look a little better," he said, walking up to her. Still grinning, he said, "Kinda weepy and vulnerable."

"Ah, now we see just what kind of woman William Henry Munro really wants."

"Only in my fantasies."

"Fantasies? Confess that to Father, do you?"

"I don't recall a commandment about fantasies." They laughed together, and it was natural, unrehearsed, as if they were old and dear friends. Quickly, though, a discomfited silence lay between them.

"If you don't need anything further from us, we're headed home," Mai said.

"Back to The Netherlands?" Her hesitation in replying was long enough for him to notice. "You will be going back to The Netherlands, won't you?" he asked.

Her expression told him nothing, and Munro suddenly felt badly for putting this temptation before her. Her response was characteristically vague.

"We'll spend a few days at our house in Virginia. Celebrate the New Year and all that. Alexei's a great cook, and I think he's planned several traditional Ukrainian dishes."

"He cooks too?"

"Everything I could want in a man."

"Yes. You've made that point."

"Oh, don't get all pouty on me, Munro. I'll send you the information on my security business. I hope you give it serious consideration."

"How often would I get to see you?"

Mai lay a hand on his cheek. "Not very often."

"You're not going back to The Hague, are you?" he asked, again. She moved her hand so her fingers held back any more comment from him. Munro took her hand in his, turned the palm to his lips, and kissed it lightly. Slowly, Mai extricated her hand then left. Munro followed her to the door and watched as she walked arm in arm with her tall husband down the hallway. Back to her life. Out of Munro's again and possibly out of her husband's again, too.

Munro smiled when she was out of sight. He looked forward to the information she would send him about a job. One thing she had taught him in their brief encounters was to never turn down an opportunity, and he wouldn't this time. His context, however, was entirely different from hers.

Y2K wasn't going to be so bad after all.

About the Author

◆

Phyllis Anne Duncan is a middle-aged Federal bureaucrat with an overactive imagination—at least that's what everyone has told her since she first started making up stories in elementary school with her weekly list of spelling words. A commercial pilot and flight instructor, she lives in Northern Virginia and publishes aviation safety information for pilots and mechanics as well as government aviation safety inspectors. In 1974 she graduated from James Madison University with a degree in History and Political Science. *Rarely Well-Behaved* is her first collection of short stories, and she hopes it will spur interest in *A Perfect Hatred*, her unpublished novel about the Oklahoma City bombing. She is currently at work on a third book, *Who is Killing the Friends of Slobodan Milosevic?*